Mastering Marissa

CYNA KADE

ELLORA'S CAVE
ROMANTICA®
WWW.ELLORASCAVE.COM

An Ellora's Cave Publication

www.ellorascave.com

Mastering Marissa

ISBN 9781419964459
ALL RIGHTS RESERVED.
Mastering Marissa Copyright © 2007 Cyna Kade
Edited by Jaynie Ritchie.
Cover artist Syneca.

Electronic book publication January 2007
Trade paperback publication 2011

MASTERING MARISSA

ৡ

Chapter One

ଛଚ

Cold metal encircled Marissa's wrists and ankles.

Heavy chains kept her motions small and constricted — not that there was anywhere to go. Her cell was barely bigger than a closet. A shower poured from the ceiling once a day. The slot at the bottom of the door spit out food twice a day and a dim version of light entered from a small window set far above her head.

How much longer could she hold out? She'd survived three days — three days alone with the walls pressing in on her. If the weight of the stones didn't crush her, he would. She shivered, rubbing her arms in a vain attempt to ease her chill as kaleidoscopic flashes of memory played in her head. Her father's assurances of safety, her friend's vehement arguments against this trip and the first sight of her captor circled in an endless loop.

The sound of a key in the door lock yanked her into the present.

Marissa backed against a wall. Still well within his reach — there simply wasn't any escape so she tilted her chin and waited for him.

Kytar opened the door wide and moved into Marissa's cell. His cedar scent enveloped her and for just a heartbeat, a false promise of freedom shimmered in the air. Clenching her jaw to fight off his allure, she stood stiffly before him.

His eyes were the color of melted dark chocolate today and a tiny sigh of relief escaped. Chocolate was good. When his eyes hardened to black, he was scary.

He took the step that put him close to her. "Are you ready, little one?"

Marissa looked up at him. A head taller and nearly twice her weight, any physical fight was futile. His strength easily overwhelmed hers and as she'd already found out, he didn't hesitate to use it. But physical combat wasn't the only way to resist.

"Answer me," he insisted, looming over her and cutting off her view of the cell and the open doorway beyond.

Marissa shook her head sending blonde curls cascading over peaked nipples. She was tempted, so tempted, by this man. She should be terrified. He'd misled her and captured her. He was ruthless and dangerous. She wanted to yell at him, but a thrill of excitement arrowed through her. Why couldn't she hate this man? What was the strange hold she felt deep inside?

For a long moment, he stared down at her. "Three days…how much longer do you think you can hold out?" he murmured, reaching out and trailing a finger down her cheek, leaving awareness in its wake.

Marissa held her breath as his finger continued down her neck and between her breasts. She closed her eyes and swallowed hard as his gentle stroke threatened to undo her self-control. Fighting off a wave of dizziness, she forced herself to breathe.

When his finger reached her chains, he hooked it in them and raised her hands up. "What will you give me if I take off the chains?"

Marissa's eyes flew open, but she stayed silent.

"Will you freely give me a kiss if I take off your chains?"

"A kiss? Just a kiss?"

"Just a kiss, little one. That's not so much to ask, is it?"

Marissa's mind circled, trying to find the catch to his generous offer. There was always a catch. He did nothing without a reason.

"What is your answer?" He tilted his head, waiting.

Marissa took a deep breath, trying to still her racing heart. Meeting his gaze, she said, "If you take off the chains—and promise to leave them off—I will give you a kiss."

He chuckled.

The seductive, tempting sound rippled through her and sank deep into her core. She wanted to lean into that sound and wrap it around her like a warm blanket. Instead, she stiffened and waited.

"Very well, little one. I will leave the chains off," he said. Reaching for the key, he opened the lock and let the chains clatter to the floor. He hesitated a moment, then cocking an eyebrow, he asked, "A second kiss for your bracelets?"

Marissa frowned. She didn't trust this new kindliness, but she wanted the bracelets off so she nodded.

He raised both eyebrows.

She forced the words past her tight throat. "Yes, a second kiss if you'll take the bracelets off—and leave them off."

He held her eyes while he freed her wrists. His thumbs rubbed her pulse points, increasing their frantic beat.

She tensed for his kisses. But he surprised her by kneeling in front of her. His head at her waist, a leather thong kept his shoulder-length, blue-black hair restrained.

He didn't say a word as he reached down and freed her feet from the chains. One more quick movement and the cold metal bracelets were gone from her ankles.

The sense of exhilaration that came with this small freedom startled her. She hadn't realized the chains and bracelets trapped her spirit, as well as her body. But she wouldn't feel gratitude, she berated herself. He still held her captive and now she owed him two kisses.

Two kisses he didn't seem in a hurry to collect.

His hands stroked her ankles, moving upward past her calves, around her knees, lingering a moment at the soft skin behind them before continuing up her thighs. Gently caressing and massaging all the way, dissipating the stiffness from her captivity.

Driving her nails into her palms, she resisted the urge to sink her fingers into his hair or to scream at him to hurry up.

When he reached the top of her thighs, he pressed to spread her legs.

"No," she said.

His hands stopped and he looked up at her. "I didn't say where the kisses would be. Spread your legs."

Marissa struggled to draw a breath.

He leaned back a little. "Are you refusing?"

Marissa's heart nearly ceased at his tone. Soft and caressing, the voice promised untold pleasure. But, she knew how easily he could—and would—follow with a demonstration of his strength. If she didn't obey him, he'd put the chains back on or force her legs apart. She had no choice. He'd trapped her once more.

With a sinking heart, she relaxed her legs and said, "No…no, I'm not refusing."

His eyes pinned her to the wall. He didn't speak again as he used a sensuous stroking motion to part her legs.

His gentle touch lulled her, weakening her knees and tension curled in her stomach. She tried to shake off his spell, but he was relentless. When he finally released her eyes, he leaned forward.

She wanted to squirm when his fingers slipped into her cleft but she stilled her motion.

His head blocked her view but she felt him even if his head hid his actions.

His hands parted her lower lips, exposing her clit to the air.

Marissa clenched her thighs. He must have felt the motion, but he ignored it while he held her open and helpless. Trembling legs sent vibrations throughout her body. She

10

pressed back against the cold stone until she felt it scrape her buttocks.

Kytar's hot breath scorched her clit and a trickle of moisture seeped down her thigh.

"You are very, very wet. You like what I'm doing, don't you, little one?"

She wanted to scream at him to get it over with, but he didn't move closer. Agonizing minutes passed as he held her open, lightly stroking her clit with a fingertip. A touch too light to release the pressure, just right though, to make her pussy throb.

In a quick motion, he stood and laughed.

A moan escaped at her unexpected release.

"Think about the fact you owe me two kisses, little one," he said, his eyes gleaming. Turning, he left her cell. The *thunk* of the door lock echoed the dropping sensation in her stomach.

She bit off a scream of frustration as her knees gave out. Hands flat on the floor, head bowed, she told herself that at least she was free of the chains. She wanted to touch herself, to ease the fire he'd built, but she wouldn't give him the satisfaction. She concentrated on stilling her breathing and calming her racing heart as she berated herself for feeling anything other than hatred.

He'd misled her, imprisoned her and frightened her. She should hate him. How could he arouse her like this? A mere glance or gentle caress was enough to have her dripping. She didn't understand his power over her. Why was it so hard to hate him? She never gave up control. She never succumbed to any man.

She was experienced, but no one had ever tormented her like this. Wasn't he ever going to satisfy the need he effortlessly created? She ached to feel him deep inside. She wanted him and it was only a matter of time before she agreed to his terms. Eventually, she'd do anything to release the throbbing tension he built higher every time she saw him.

How could she fight him when she'd never met a man like him? Nothing in her previous life prepared her for a Darinthian male.

She'd been foolish to think she could safely seek her family on this vile planet. She'd been so arrogant, so confident and so wrong. She wanted to forget but memories flooded her. She remembered each point where she might have changed her fate, especially the beginning—her mother's death recently.

The funeral service was small. Her stepfather was there, of course. The only other people attending were Marissa and Shelley, Marissa's best friend.

After the service, Marissa turned to leave, but her stepfather stepped in front of her. "She left you nothing."

"At least you can't hurt her anymore," Marissa bit out.

"She liked what I did. Maybe you'd like a taste of me, now that she's gone."

Marissa glared up at him. She'd never understood why her mother—beautiful and talented—had bound herself to such despicable slime. Small and petty, he delighted in vicious little actions that denigrated her mother. Every time Marissa saw bruises on her mother's arms or face, she'd beg her mother to leave.

Her mother had merely smiled and said, "Someday you'll understand."

Now her mother was gone and Marissa would never understand.

Marissa didn't answer her stepfather, merely stepped around him. With her mother gone, she never had to talk to him again.

He called to her retreating back, "Your mother always was an inconsiderate whore."

Marissa whirled, fists clenched, but Shelley stepped in front of her. "He's not worth it. Don't let him provoke you."

Marissa bit back a heated reply and let Shelley lead her away. On the trip home, Marissa's anger leaked away, leaving her empty. Shelley cast worried glances her way and Marissa wasn't surprised when Shelley insisted on coming into the apartment.

"You shouldn't be alone right now. Why don't you come home with me?" Shelley said as she made tea.

"I'll be okay. I just need some space and I'll be okay." Shelley just didn't understand how lost Marissa felt. With the death of her mother, she was alone in the galaxy. She'd always be alone now. She had no other blood relatives and much as she liked Shelley's family, they weren't *her* family.

A week later, she returned home from work to find a package from her mother's lawyer. She frowned as she broke the seals. Her mother had died destitute. Her stepfather had seen to that. What could the lawyers want with her?

The only thing inside the package was a thin envelope, addressed in her mother's handwriting. A sad smile broke across Marissa's face as she saw the paper rather than a vid. Her mother always hated vids.

"*Someday I will tell you everything.*"

Marissa heard the voice from the past clearly, as if her mother was standing beside her. Her hands shook as she opened the envelope and pulled out the letter. She sank to the floor as she began to read.

My darling,

I don't know how to break this to you, so I will simply tell you. Your biological father is Darinthian. I've never stopped loving him. His name is Davo Kraj. He knows of your existence. He wants to meet you. Please contact him. Please, travel to Darinth and meet your family. He will keep you safe. I think you will like the planet and surrounded by your family you will find a freedom you never expected.

All my love, always,

Mom

Marissa wasn't sure how long she sat on the floor, stunned by the revelation that not only had her mother been on Darinth, but also that she'd fallen in love there.

Shelley found her still sitting on the floor with the letter in her hand.

"Marissa?"

She looked up, eyes blank with shock.

Shelley frowned and gently took the letter from Marissa's hand. Her eyes widened as she read it. "Darinthian. Your father is Darinthian?"

"Apparently," Marissa said in a barely audible voice. Her hand shook as she reached out and let Shelley help her up.

"You can't go to Darinth. The men are bastards. Just last night, the news vid showed a Darinthian clip full of chained, naked females. The men demanded submission and got it. Females have no rights on Darinth."

"I have no intention of going to Darinth, but—"

"But nothing," interrupted Shelley. "They specifically warned single females not to travel to the planet. I don't know why the galactic council allows Darinthian practices to continue. They're barbarians."

Marissa shrugged.

Darinth was the primary supplier of amoulian, a necessary component for space travel. Simple economics won over the rights of females. Oh, the galactic council issued warnings and forced Darinthian customs officials to get a signed release from single females traveling to the planet. But otherwise, male domination continued and the men of Darinth were free to practice their customs without restraint or interference.

"What are you going to do?" Shelley asked. "Are you going to contact him?"

"I don't know."

At twenty-five, Marissa considered herself sexually experienced. She liked sex. Petite and cute—not beautiful, but glowing with energy—she never lacked partners. Her long, dirty blonde hair and cat green eyes effortlessly lured men and she enjoyed experimenting. She enjoyed the physical release men provided. But Darinthian sexual practices were far different from anything she'd ever experienced. Darinthian customs horrified her. They were too close to the things her stepfather had done to her mother.

She'd watched her mother's subjugation and vowed she'd stay free and independent. She never let a man take control, not that any man had ever been strong enough to claim control. The thought of placing herself in the hands of any male, much less a Darinthian male, left her trembling with anger. But how could she ignore the fact she had a family?

For days, her mother's letter filled her mind. When had her mother been on Darinth? Why hadn't her mother told her? Why had her mother hidden her father's existence? How could she ask Marissa to go to the planet? How could she not go? The idea of family haunted her, but the fact that family was on Darinth chilled her.

Before Marissa could decide what to do about the letter, her father took the initiative and surprised her with a comm call.

"I just heard of your mother's death. I share your grief."

Marissa's eyes filled with tears at his simple words. She drew comfort from the fact that someone else grieved her mother's death, even if he was Darinthian. Her mother had once loved this man and he obviously loved her mother. He was her father, she reminded herself. She wasn't alone in the galaxy.

"I knew of your existence," he continued, "but I respected your mother's wishes. She didn't want you to know about me."

"Why?" Marissa asked. "Why did she hide you from me?"

"She had her reasons," he replied. "Those reasons are too complex to discuss during an interplanetary call. Come visit," he encouraged Marissa.

"Can't we meet off-planet...I've heard Darinth is not a place for single females..." Marissa hesitated.

"You'd be under my protection, not single. Please, Marissa, my business is such that I can't go off-planet," he replied. "If we are to meet, it must be here. You needn't worry. I'll keep you safe," he promised.

Although Marissa believed him, the thought of traveling voluntarily to a place that subjugated women kept her from saying yes.

Over the next few weeks, she and her father continued their communication. He didn't fit the image she'd built up of the males on Darinth. He looked like the elder statesman he was and he was intelligent, funny and kind. Every time they spoke, his concern for her well-being came through. She could feel his love, even though he'd never met her in person. She longed to hug him but she continued to say no, she wouldn't go Darinth.

Despite her decision, she tried to find out more about the planet. Mystery shrouded Darinth. She couldn't find any educational vids, just sensational ones like Shelley had seen and of course, the famed sex vids. She and Shelley had rented some.

The vids reinforced her decision. Marissa had never realized there were so many ways to hurt a female body. The women screamed in pain, while the men laughed and intensified their assaults. The vids nauseated and sickened Marissa — they brought back memories of her mother's hell.

The next time her father invited her to Darinth, Marissa shook her head. "I've seen the vids. I won't go to Darinth."

"The vids?" He frowned. "You mean the ones we export?"

Marissa nodded.

Her father's face lightened and his lips twitched as if fighting off a smile. He waved a hand, saying, "Those vids are simply to make money. They don't represent us at all. They cater to the prurient interests of the rest of the galaxy."

"They were horrible."

"Yes, they are but they don't accurately portray our customs. If you've been watching those vids, I certainly understand your fear. If you really want to know about Darinthian customs, I'll send you some local vids, the ones we watch."

Marissa didn't respond to his offer. She cringed at the idea of her own father sending her sex vids.

Her father searched her face for another moment, finally saying, "Our sexual practices are not shameful. They are integral to our culture and worthy of respect." Then, changing the subject, he told her another story about a relative she'd never met.

Marissa forgot her father's offer until a package arrived.

Chapter Two

စာ

"I won't watch a woman's enslavement," Marissa told Davo the next time they spoke.

"Marissa, you know nothing of our customs. I've dealt with many off-worlders. I know how they view our practices. I know about the rumors. We let those rumors circulate unanswered because our customs are sacred, not fodder for common discussion. Watch the vid and learn. Or would you rather judge us based on gossip?"

Marissa didn't answer him, but all the next day, his question troubled her. Was she judging Darinth unfairly? He'd called their practices sacred, but that didn't make them right. She spent the evening casting numerous glances at the package she'd thrown in a corner. She wanted to trash it but her inherent fairness wouldn't let her. She sighed. She had to play the vid. She owed her father a chance to justify his customs. She picked up the package. Breaking the seals, she inserted it into her vid player.

The vid opened with a naked woman chained against a wall. A silvery steel collar circled her throat. Her arms stretched straight up and the same silvery metal fastened around her wrists, holding them tight. On her tiptoes, her legs spread wide and held by more of the silvery metal. Her shaved pubis revealed her glistening cunt. It was obscene.

Marissa reached for the control to flick off the vid when a man moved into view. Her breath caught at his rugged masculinity and she forgot about turning the vid off as his image seared into her brain.

His cock thrust nearly to his waist. Larger than any she'd ever seen, she clenched her thighs as she imagined being penetrated by such a weapon and held in his strong arms.

He towered over the chained woman. But the visual didn't frighten Marissa, she was too captivated by his soft expression. A hint of a smile played at his lips and humor glinted in his eyes as he asked, "Are you ready?"

Her glistening lips parted into a needy pout. "More than ready. I need you," she said in a sultry voice. "I need you now, please just take me."

His face burst into a full-blown smile. "Not quite yet, darling."

Marissa's body heated as she wondered what he'd do to the vulnerable woman spread open before him. She didn't have long to wait for an answer.

The man reached out and gently captured the woman's breasts, carefully leaving her nipples free. Marissa could see his small movements, massaging the breasts in his strong fingers, forearms flexing with each movement. The woman's nipples filled, stretching out as if begging for a touch. But the man ignored them.

What it would be like to be helpless in that man's hands? He obviously knew how to arouse a woman. No wonder the woman quickly progressed to screams of need, begging the man to satisfy her.

Marissa wanted to turn off the vid, but the man held her as easily as he held his prisoner. Molten heat raced through Marissa's veins, in time with her heart, as moisture seeped from her aching pussy. Riveted, she watched the entire vid.

Not once did he hurt the woman. Not once did he do anything other than pleasure her. The man teased and caressed his helpless victim until she was squirming and begging. The woman's pleading escalated, becoming one long demand for release.

The man laughed at the woman's pleading, telling her, "Darling, we've barely started." He tortured her by ignoring her exhortations. Repeatedly he brought her near her peak and denied her final release.

Marissa didn't think she could stand to watch the woman's frustration any longer, when the man finally made a quick flicking motion directly on the woman's clit. The resulting orgasm tightened every muscle in the woman's body and it seemed to go on forever.

The second time Marissa watched the vid her hand crept to her burning clit. Using a fingertip, she tapped on the erect nub and squirmed under her own ministrations as she wished she wasn't alone. Her orgasm washed over her in a quick flash. Too quick. It wasn't until the third viewing that Marissa delayed her own satisfaction. Holding off wasn't just frustrating. It intensified her own pleasure, much as it had intensified the captive woman's pleasure.

None of the men Marissa knew could or would do those things to her. She'd never met a man satisfied to hold off on his own pleasure while he concentrated on hers. The vids didn't just excite her—they also disturbed her. The women gave up control to earn their satisfaction. And that fact cooled Marissa's ardor. No man controlled her.

The next time her father called, he asked about the vid.

Marissa, angry at her arousal, spit out, "I watched it."

"What did you think of it?"

Marissa shook her head, firmly keeping her face impassive unable to prevent the heat in her cheeks.

Her father eyed her closely. "I'm sorry. I didn't mean to embarrass you. That was a public vid though, broadcast just last month. Sex is freely discussed on Darinth, but I do understand your customs are very different." Then, thankfully, he changed the subject.

But the next week another vid arrived.

Marissa wanted to scream in frustration. How could she watch another vid of a woman having sex? She wanted to throw it out, along with the haunting idea of Darinthian sex. It must be fiction. The vids couldn't possibly depict real sexual acts. Men like that just didn't exist, she told herself firmly, even as she gave in and started the vid.

This one opened with a woman tied to a table. Multiple straps crossed her extremities, with one wide strap at her waist and a smaller one circling her throat. The special table that had split supports for the woman's thighs. The supports angled wide, allowing a close camera shot of the woman's gaping lower lips. She glistened with moisture despite the harsh-looking clamp that held the woman's clit erect.

Marissa cringed at the sight of the clamp and wondered how the woman stood the pain. The clamp didn't seem at all erotic but the woman's pussy dripped with arousal. Was the woman a masochist? Did she get off on pain?

The camera panned over the woman, slowly, as if it were a hand caressing her. Marissa saw matching clamps on the woman's nipples, nipples that were gloriously erect just waiting for a touch.

Marissa didn't stop to think before pinching her own nipples. It hurt. How could the woman stand the clamps?

Gagged and blindfolded, this woman was obviously more helpless than the last. At least the woman in the previous vid had been able to scream out her need.

Once again, Marissa was just reaching out to turn the vid off when a man entered.

This man was fully dressed in loose-fitting pants and a red sleeveless tunic. Despite his clothes, Marissa saw that he was every bit as powerful as the man in the last vid. He moved with the same masculine grace and control too. He walked to the woman's side and stood over her. His hand trailed along her abdomen, ignoring the clamps and the begging nipples. The woman's moan was loud, despite the gag in her mouth.

21

A violent longing rushed through Marissa and just for an instant, she imagined herself to be that woman, helpless under the man's touch.

Marissa nearly exploded with need as the man teased the woman, forcing her close to the peak then pulling her back— controlling her arousal as easily as he controlled her body.

Marissa's finger crept down to her slit. She sighed with pleasure as her fingers delved into her moist heat. She tried to hold off, to wait for the woman, but she just didn't have the patience or discipline to ignore her needs. She exploded once and then again when the man ripped the clamps off the woman and the woman arched in ecstasy.

The next day, she cringed in memory. Wasn't there something perverted in her father sending her this kind of vid? He said it was a public broadcast. She shook her head. Just how different were Darinthian customs?

Even more uncomfortable was the fact the vids fascinated her. The vids should horrify her. These women were helpless even if they didn't seem like victims, even if they appeared excited and happy under a man's control. How could they surrender like that?

Marissa didn't understand why the vids aroused her to a fevered pitch of need. She'd lusted before but never anything like this. She hadn't known she could be so aroused and that was just by watching. What would happen if she surrendered to a man like that? What was she thinking? She'd never surrender to one of those men. But the vids captivated her and she kept watching.

She watched the vid again and again, pleasing herself, but still aching with need. Masturbation didn't satisfy her. She felt empty and unlike the women in the vids, she felt unloved. Maybe she'd just been too long without sex.

The next night, she debated calling an ex-boyfriend. He'd never held off though and despite his gentleness, he'd never really satisfied her. Why bother? She turned back to the two vids, unable to resist their allure.

She didn't know how much longer she could hold out against her father's exhortations to visit the planet. Not that she'd necessarily have sex with a Darinthian male, she told herself. Her desire to visit the planet had nothing to do with sex.

She wanted to meet her family. That was the only reason she'd consider such a trip. Besides, her father had repeatedly told her she'd be safe. She trusted him, didn't she? Still Marissa hesitated.

Then the third vid arrived.

The third vid was even more erotic than the first two. Marissa's brain jangled as she tried to reconcile the woman's blissful response to pain with her own horror of it. Marissa, witness to too much of her stepfather's cruelty, was certain that pain was a bad thing. But the woman's reaction stuck in her head. Clearly, the woman in the vid didn't feel that pain was bad.

No actress could fake the screaming orgasm that had bowed her back into a rigid arch. The woman liked pain. That much was obvious.

Marissa wanted to be angry. She wanted to say the woman was a slave, an abused slave, yet, how could she dismiss the clenching ache she felt as she'd watched the man's strong arm slash down with the crop and listened to the woman's moans?

Each slash left a red line on the woman's ass, until it bloomed into a flowering pattern of red, pink and white. Moisture dripped down the woman's thigh and Marissa's own heat rose. A secret part of her wondered how she'd perform in the same situation.

The man's face was riveting. Intent on the woman, oblivious to his own arousal, he focused entirely on his partner's responses. Marissa saw his concern when he finished the woman's beating. Every line of his body spoke of love not anger.

Marissa was still flushed with desire when she heard her comm chime. She took a few deep breaths, stilling her racing heart before moving to answer it.

Her father took one look at her face and said, "Did I interrupt something?"

Marissa's jaw tightened. How could he tell so easily? Fighting embarrassment, she said, "Stop sending the vids."

He shrugged and smiled, "I'm not forcing you to watch them. But now you've seen how Darinthian males cherish their females, how can you still be afraid to visit?"

Marissa closed her eyes and took in a deep breath. Her heart raced as she asked, "You mean it never goes beyond what the vids show? That's not what is said about Darinth."

Her father shrugged again. "Some males might go further but never without their companion's consent. Every male cares for his companion. Along with domination comes responsibility. Can't you see the men's concern for their companions?"

"Women are not property. They wouldn't need care if the men weren't abusing them."

"You really think what you've seen is abuse?"

Marissa hesitated as a vivid image of a woman pleading for more pain flashed into her mind, accompanied by the woman's screams of ecstasy.

"What you've seen is a sacred rite on Darinth, an expression of sexual compatibility, not abuse."

"Sacred rite?"

"The vids show various binding rituals."

"Sex is a religion?"

"Not quite, but definitely sacred to us."

"And it's public? That's too creepy!"

"Aren't most sacred ceremonies public? We all rejoice in the binding."

Marissa stared at the vid screen. Her father seemed angry with her, but his beliefs were wrong. "I can't, I won't do those things."

Her father sighed and his anger—if that's what it was—leaked away. "You don't have to do anything. You'll be under my protection. You'll be safe. You never need experience any sex on Darinth if you choose not to."

Marissa didn't answer, stunned by the flash of disappointment that flooded her at his words. She realized that a part of her wanted to submit, to test her will and explore her needs. How could she want to be a slave? She cringed, her cheeks flooding with warmth.

"No male can do anything without your permission," he continued.

"But according to planetary law, my presence on the planet is permission," she said, fighting her response to the vids.

Her father sighed. "Marissa, you're my daughter. I yearn to kiss your cheek and hug you. We've lost so much over the years. Please don't deny us time together because you're afraid of something that might not ever happen. Besides, your mother survived her experiences on the planet. You told me she left you a letter and that she wanted you to visit. Will you ignore her wishes?"

There was that, mused Marissa.

Before she could frame a reply, her father continued, "Marissa, I want to meet you. But as I've told you, there are always challenges to power and our family is one of the most powerful on the planet. I am the dominant male in our family. Dominants never leave the planet. Doing so would leave the family vulnerable to attack. I simply cannot walk away from my duties and responsibilities. Surely, you understand."

Marissa did understand. She admired her father for his stand. If she had a family, she'd do anything to protect them too. He'd told her of her half-brothers, half-sisters, uncles, aunts, nephews, nieces and cousins. The thought of meeting and belonging ate at her control.

A whole family was waiting to welcome her, if only she could overcome her fears. She admitted she was lonely. On Darinth, she would not be alone. Her mother's last wish was that Marissa visit the planet. Could she ignore that wish?

How had her mother survived Darinth? Marissa didn't have the answer to that question but if her mother had survived then she could too, couldn't she?

"Please come for a visit. I will keep you safe," Davo said.

Her thoughts tangled in a confused web of desire and longing. She knew the only way to untangle them was to visit the planet. She felt no desire to continue refusing. She wanted to meet Davo, in person. She needed to touch him and feel him. "I'll visit if you promise I'll be safe," she said, giving up her fight.

"Just wait for me in the arrival area. Don't pass customs without me. Then you'll be under my protection and I'll keep you safe."

* * * * *

Preparations for the trip took a few weeks. She had plenty of vacation time, so that wasn't a problem. Packing and travel plans were easily made. Overcoming Shelley's concerns had not been so easy though.

Shelley hadn't supported Marissa's decision to visit Darinth. Indeed, she'd been loud and vocal in her opposition to the trip.

"Marissa," she said, "they'll make you a slave! How can you agree to walk into such a situation?"

Marissa frowned down at her suitcase. Her decision made, she wasn't going to change her mind now. "My father has guaranteed my safety. They won't make me a slave."

Shelley frowned at Marissa's back. "I've talked to some men who've been to Darinth. They said they'd never seen such submissive females. They told me some of the things the men ordered women to do and that the women obeyed without question. Marissa, they whipped women and the women begged for more." Shelley shook her head, red curls flying. "You're too independent for a place like Darinth. The men there are serious about domination. Besides, if anything goes wrong, I won't be able to help you," Shelley continued her theme of warning.

Finally, Marissa yelled, "Enough! That's enough! I am going. My father wants to see me and I want to see him. I want to meet the family I never knew I had. My father promised to keep me safe and I believe him. I'm going."

* * * * *

Marissa arrived on Darinth late at night. The transport docked earlier than expected, so she wasn't surprised that her father wasn't there yet. She'd just have to wait. She followed her father's directions, staying in the arrival section and not passing through customs. The first two hours passed slowly as stood with her back against a wall, waiting for her father.

The arrival center was a large room without amenities. Meant as a transit point, not a waiting area, there were no chairs, no bathrooms and no food. Marissa was tired from the trip and anxious to find a resting place.

She noted with unease that she was the only woman in the room. Large, harsh-looking Darinthian males stared at her with speculative gleams of appraisal as they passed by. She felt nervous and naked before their roving eyes. She wasn't used to confident men coldly evaluating her body as if they could see beneath her clothes and find her every flaw.

One man had been audacious enough to stop right in front of her.

Reaching out, he'd cupped her chin and asked, "Do you need a male?"

Marissa, startled and angered by his question, pulled back from his touch. She nearly screamed, but she held on to her self-control and answered firmly. "No!"

"That's regretful. I would like to tame you," he said.

Her face flamed beneath his gaze. Then he laughed and walked away.

Marissa watched him walk out of the center, not relaxing until he had passed customs. His brash actions and words had frightened her.

He was the only man who talked to her, but every man that passed by looked at her with the same speculative gleam.

Marissa wanted to yell at the Darinthians. Why couldn't they be more like the men on her world? Kind and courteous, the men on her world would never stare until her face flamed. But the Darinthians were so different, she didn't dare yell. She didn't know what they'd do. So she stayed quiet, trying to blend into the wall and disappear.

If only there was a place to curl up and hide, but the arrival room was bare and her position against a wall hid nothing. These men made her feel naked and helpless and she began to understand why women needed protectors on this planet. Her nerves wouldn't let her sit on the floor, so she stood, waiting for her father. Where was he?

Chapter Three

ഇ

Marissa squirmed as she waited in the arrival center. Her emotions fluctuated. One minute she wanted to spit in anger, the next she wanted to cringe in terror. How dare these men frighten her? Their bold stares made her feel small and exposed, like a tempting morsel they could easily gobble up. She wanted to crawl into a hole to escape their knowing eyes. Nausea threatened and she swallowed trying to force her stomach to behave. Where was her father?

Finally, one of the customs officials approached. His stare was as brash as all the others as he walked toward her. He too was at least a head taller than Marissa. Were all Darinthian men so tall? She didn't see any ugly men either. All the men were muscular, some more than others, but they all had the same masculine grace and beauty as the men in the vids.

Uncertain whether she longed to gaze at their beauty or run from their glittering eyes, they reminded Marissa of large predators—beautiful but powerful, silent, quick and deadly. She felt petite and helpless for the first time in her life and she didn't like the feeling. She struggled to breathe at the thought of being under the care of any of these men.

The customs official stepped close. In a cold voice he asked, "Why aren't you going through customs? Do you have something to hide?"

"I'm meeting someone," she replied. "My father told me to wait here."

"Who is your father?" he demanded.

Seeing no harm in telling him, she replied.

Marissa saw a flash of recognition at the name. Her father held a position in the ruling council. She wasn't surprised that the customs official recognized the name. She was surprised when his eyes traveled her body, inventorying her assets, as if her powerful father made her more interesting, rather than off-limits.

He finished his perusal then nodded and said, "I will notify the appropriate person of your arrival."

Marissa noticed the strange wording, but trembling with exhaustion, she dismissed it as just a language difference.

Fifteen minutes later, Marissa's world tilted. Her eyes locked on a man who'd just entered the arrival center and she couldn't pull them away. Her nipples tightened and her pussy ached. She was shocked at her urge to jump the man. Yes, he was gorgeous, but every Darinthian male she'd seen was gorgeous. He didn't seem outwardly different from the others.

Shoulder-length dark hair framed a hard face—all angles and planes—an uncompromising face. A sleeveless shirt highlighted powerful biceps and forearms. A black two-inch wide belt circled his waist. His tight, dark pants did little to hide equally powerful thighs and what lay between them.

Why did this man wreak havoc with her libido? She longed to have him hold her and she wondered what his lips would taste like. How could she respond to him like this? She didn't even know him. But her eyes remained fixed on him as he paused to talk to the customs agent. Taller than the customs official the man bent down a little as they exchanged words.

Marissa started when the agent pointed at her.

The stranger looked over at her and flares of tension arced between them as their eyes met. He held her for a moment longer before boldly raking his eyes over her body. His gaze didn't make her feel naked and she wondered if his arms could possibly be as hard as they looked or if his cock could be that impossibly large.

She stood a little straighter, tilting her chin as she returned his stare. She wouldn't let this man intimidate her. He had no right to examine her.

At her movement, his lips tilted in a half-smile as if he heard her thoughts. His eyes seemed to burn black. She mentally shook herself. People didn't have black eyes. It must be a trick of the lighting or exhaustion. She struggled to maintain her position. She wouldn't sag in front of this man.

She wanted to look away from him, to ignore him, but the force of his presence held her in thrall. It wasn't until he turned back to the clerk that she could look elsewhere. In her peripheral vision, she saw him hand something to the clerk.

Marissa stared off into the distance aware of his slow stroll toward her. He closed the distance, until he stood close, very close. Too close, but with the wall at her back, he blocked her escape.

Well, if she couldn't retreat, there was nothing left to do but be brave.

She looked up at him and his eyes captured hers. She'd been wrong, His eyes weren't black. They were the color of dark chocolate, melted and liquid, inviting sinful exploration. His presence seemed to suck out all her air but there were benefits. He easily blocked her vision of the other men in the arrival center.

"My name is Kytar. I am here to pick you up," he said.

His deep and husky voice reverberated in her chest, sending out tendrils of warmth, wrapping her in his protection. She longed to sink into the safety of his arms, to feel his fingers tangling in her hair and holding her close.

With a sharp gasp, she fought back to reality. What was she thinking? She shook off her fascination. There was nothing to like about a Darinthian male, she told herself sternly. Stiffening her back, she said, "You're not my father."

"No, but I am here to pick you up."

"My father told me to wait for him...not to go with anyone else," Marissa said.

A black flash, like a warning flare, flicked through his eyes. But it was gone before she really saw it. Then he smiled,

31

stunning Marissa. The smile softened his hard face, heating his deep brown eyes and deepening the smile lines around his mouth and eyes. His blue-black hair shimmered in the room's light and though he towered over Marissa, his stance softened becoming protective rather than threatening.

"I promise you I will take good care of you, but if you'd prefer to wait here," he shrugged and moved back to gesture to the cold, forbidding surroundings, "I will wait with you. You should not be here alone."

"My father said I'd be safe here."

He slanted a glance down at her. The half-smile curled his lips again. "Did he? And do you feel safe here?"

Marissa wasn't going to answer that question. Telling this dangerous man she felt threatened not only by the others, but by him as well, seemed unwise. Instead, she asked, "Did my father send you?"

"I came because of your father," he replied smoothly.

"Where is my father?"

"He's been detained. Your father is a very important man. He has many responsibilities. I'll escort you, if you let me," Kytar said, never losing his look of warm concern.

Marissa, mindful of her father's warnings, shifted her feet and said, "I'd rather wait a little longer."

Marissa expected a protest, but he simply said, "As you wish."

Another hour crept by. Marissa longed to sink to the floor and curl up. Her exhaustion made it difficult to focus on anything. She'd tried to talk to Kytar thinking that talk might help keep her awake, but when she asked how he knew her father, he merely said, "I've known your father all my life."

All her other questions were answered with similar terseness, silently rebuking her. Apparently, Darinthian woman didn't ask questions. His frown deepened a little with each question until the weight of his disapproval grew to a point where she finally fell silent.

Kytar stood, perfectly still, seemingly content to wait with her. His cedar scent reminded her of campfires and high pine forests. He smelled like the outdoors, increasing her desire to leave the arrival center. She drew in his soothing scent every time she took a breath. Lulled, she leaned back against the wall and closed her eyes, just for a moment. She hadn't realized she was tired enough to dream while still standing.

An image of the bulge of his cock, hidden under his pants, flooded her mind. Thighs clenched as she saw him in a scene from one of the vids. Built like the men in the vids he easily slipped into the role. She nearly felt his cock in her mouth, even while wondering how she'd take something so large. The image of Kytar, naked beneath her mouth and hands, brought her back to awareness with a start.

Her face flamed as she looked up to find Kytar staring down intently. Could he read her thoughts? Or smell her arousal? Too bad straight-up vanilla sex wouldn't be his style. He'd take control, whether she wanted to give it or not. She mentally shook herself, forcing the images of Kytar from her mind.

Another hour passed. Marissa's escort remained silent though his very presence seemed to warn the other men away. They still looked, but when they noticed Kytar, they nodded to him and stopped examining her. Marissa sighed and leaned back against the wall again. Where was her father?

Kytar ached. The beauty of the petite blonde standing next to him went straight to his gut. He'd been rock-hard since his first glimpse of her. He wanted to grab her. Grab her, bind her and collar her, making his claim known to every other male. The connection between them, though unexpected, was unmistakable. The magic beat at him, demanding he start the binding ritual. He itched to comply, but he couldn't, not yet, he told himself, fighting off the urge.

He glanced down. Standing proudly, fighting exhaustion, she was a defiant little thing. He'd linked with many women, but no Darinthian woman had ever fought him beyond a token resistance. He hadn't realized that a woman's defiance would inflame him. And the very fact she'd obeyed her father and said no to leaving, excited him. It meant she was trainable. He knew she'd fight. She wasn't used to Darinthian customs, she'd fight. He nearly laughed aloud. Her fighting would be useless.

He welcomed the opportunity to tame an off-worlder. Such opportunities were rare. Her defiance was intoxicating, like a bottle of rich wine. He'd already inventoried her many assets.

She'd piled her blonde curls on top of her head, hiding its length. He wanted to find out how long her hair was. Once she was in his power, the first thing he'd do was pull it down. He hoped it flowed far down her back. Her green eyes flashed with life and her lush mouth seemed made for his cock.

Her clothes revealed more than they hid. Her breasts were a perfect handful. They were natural too. He was glad to see they were natural, without the revealing ridge of augmented breasts. Natural breasts responded better. She had a waist he could circle with his hands. Her hips seemed almost too small for him, but she would take him. He would fit.

Her light floral scent wafted over him, reminding him of the lilacs surrounding his house. Her scent beat at him, calling to him and increasing his eagerness. He wanted to take her home. And he would, he just needed to rein in his impatience.

If he rushed her, she'd bolt. He wouldn't lose her. Her capture was integral to his plans. He'd have her soon enough. Though he hadn't expected a connection, it really didn't interfere with his plans. Everything was proceeding nicely. There was no need to rush. He just had to wait her out. Marissa didn't know it but her father wasn't coming. Eventually, her own needs would force her to agree to leave with him.

Kytar didn't try to convince Marissa to leave, he merely stood patiently next to her. Because he didn't press her to leave, her guard fell just a little. She grew more tired with each passing moment. Her legs ached. Her back throbbed. She wanted nothing more than to sit down for a few moments and she needed the facilities. Where was her father?

She finally asked, "Is there any place I can wash my hands?"

"I'm sorry. Not in the arrival center," he replied.

Marissa squirmed, wishing she hadn't drunk that last glass of juice.

"I will protect you," he said, slanting a glance downward, never raising his voice above a whisper. "You suffer needlessly."

Marissa looked up to find his eyes locked on her face. She didn't see any sign of ruthless domination or cruelty, just warm concern.

"My father told me not to leave without him."

"Your father cares about your well-being. He would not want you to suffer."

Marissa's face flamed. Her need was growing urgent. How embarrassing that Kytar should know. "How much longer is my father going to be?"

Kytar shrugged. "There's no way of telling."

Marissa groaned and suffered through another half-hour. Still there was no sign of her father. "Can't we call him?"

Kytar slanted another glance down at her. "Your father is dealing with revolutionaries in a small country. If he leaves the council before the situation resolves many are likely to die. Would you have him abandon his responsibilities?"

She shook her head. "Of course not, but I'm not certain..." she trailed off, unable to give voice to her need. It was just too embarrassing.

Kytar turned and moved in front of her again. A fresh wave of cedar washed over her. He tucked a finger under her chin and gently raised her head. Gazing deeply into her eyes, he said, "I understand your fear. I respect the fact you are obeying your father but I repeat that he would not want you to suffer. You are tired and probably hungry and thirsty. You have needs to meet. Leave with me and I will keep you safe."

Marissa closed her eyes. His tender voice lulled her. She couldn't fight her exhaustion much longer and he seemed so sure of himself. He did make her feel safe, even as he frightened her, she reminded herself. How could he do both at once? One feeling was false, but which one?

Unfortunately, her bodily functions demanded attention. Either she left now or she'd have a very embarrassing accident. She had to leave with him. She had no choice. Sighing, she shoved aside her misgivings and reluctantly nodded. "Okay."

"Do you leave with me willingly?" he asked in that inviting voice that reverberated through her heart.

"Yes, I'm leaving with you willingly. Let's go," she replied. Her decision made, she dismissed the fleeting stir of caution that raced through her mind. She was just too tired to listen and she had to find the facilities soon.

Kytar rewarded her statement with a warm smile. "I'll take care of you," he said as he gently guided her through customs.

Marissa stopped at the customs desk. "I won't sign a release."

The agent smiled, waving his hands. "No need for a release. You're under the protection of a male." He smiled at Kytar, a satisfied expression on his face.

Marissa hesitated. She didn't understand the glance they exchanged. She wanted to pause to figure it out, but Kytar gently pulled her along and she dismissed the glance as a male thing, of no consequence to her.

Kytar led her to a room just outside the customs station. "I'll wait here," he said.

A few moments later, Marissa came back out. Now that she could pull her mind out of her bladder, she could hear screaming warnings in her head. She hesitated, looking back toward the arrival center.

"Your father hasn't arrived," Kytar said, as if once more reading her mind.

Marissa nodded, but she was uncomfortable with her decision to leave with Kytar. She could see the dawn, just beginning, through the large windows of the center. Her father had told her to stay at the arrival center, but she'd stayed all night and he hadn't shown up. Where was he? Why had he sent a stranger? Kytar's commanding presence now seemed more threatening than reassuring. "Maybe I should just wait here..."

Once more, a black flash moved through his eyes before they melted back to chocolate. "You agreed to place your safety with me."

How did his eyes change colors like that? But Marissa dismissed the question as his words penetrated. She frowned. "I don't remember agreeing to that."

She started to pull back from him but his hand circled her arm in a firm grip.

"You agreed to leave with me—willingly. On Darinth, that's a request for protection."

"Wait a minute—"

Kytar cut off her protest by tangling his fingers in her hair and pulling her close. His mouth descended on hers. The kiss started slow, but quickly escalated into a demand for satisfaction. His tongue sought entry, refusing to stop at her closed lips, he licked the seam of her mouth until she gasped for air and his tongue entered in a swift stroke.

His arm at her waist kept her close while he leisurely explored her moist recess and danced with her tongue.

Marissa's knees went weak as a surge of heat flashed through her body. Kytar ground her close enough to feel his erection — an erection she wanted planted deep inside. What was happening to her? She'd never suffered an attack of lust like this. What was it with this guy? How did her arouse her so easily?

She panted when he broke the kiss, finally whispering, "I want to wait for my father. I don't want to go with you."

His lips brushed her hair. "It is too late to retreat. You've placed your safety in my hands. You'll come with me."

She struggled to escape but his arm was a steel band around her waist, unmovable, holding her tight against his body. His penis throbbed against her, as if demanding entrance. Once more, a wave of arousal swept her body and she longed to surrender to its demand.

Instead, she fought for the breath that his closeness seemed to steal. "No! My father —"

"Your father is not here. I am. I had hoped to bind you in private, but…" He shrugged.

Marissa's knees weakened under the onslaught of his soft words. Her head shook as if she could deny reality. Eyes burning, she arched her head to look at him.

"You are mine," he said, smiling down with satisfaction.

"No!" she screamed and struggled to escape his hard grip but he held her easily, even when she tried to kick him.

"Stop fighting," he commanded.

"No!"

"Stop fighting or not only will I bind you, I'll collar you here in front of everyone. Is that what you want? A public demonstration of my complete mastery over you?"

Marissa stilled at his words, the lump in her throat preventing any words.

"I'm trying to make allowances for you. But you accepted my offer of companionship when you accepted my offer of safety," he whispered in her ear.

"I won't be a slave!"

"I am not enslaving you. I offer companionship."

"Semantics, slave or companion, it is the same thing."

"Didn't your father teach you anything? Companionship is an honorable position on Darinth."

"Let me go!"

"No, little one," he replied. "I won't let you escape."

Marissa yelped in surprise, as he forced her arms behind her back. Crossing her wrists, he tightly bound them with leather thongs and roughly pushed her to her knees. Stunned by his sudden movements, her lips still burning from his heated kiss, Marissa stared up at him.

His deep, dark eyes met hers. No longer warm and brown, his eyes had darkened to onyx and glittered with cold satisfaction.

"I won't—" she started to say.

He interrupted by forcing a foot between her legs and kicking her knees farther apart. "You will." A smile crossed his face. "You have no tools to fight me, no weapons. You are like a virgin on this planet. You don't know what you face."

"No!"

Ignoring her protest, he tugged out her hair ties.

Freed, her hair spilled down her back, like a golden waterfall nearly reaching her waist. Then he wrapped her hair around his hand and forced her head back.

Still on her knees, his firm grip extended her neck, forcing her to look up the long line of his body.

"I know you're not accustomed to our ways. That fact saves you from my anger, but I will not allow this senseless resistance to continue. You are mine," he said. Taking a deep breath, his voice slowed and deepened. "I claim you as mine.

You are my companion. I own your body. I own your mind. I own your spirit. I claim you as mine."

A shudder ripped through Marissa as he recited the ritualistic-sounding words. She gasped as invisible bands tightened in a ball deep inside. Warmth pooled in her belly, moisture dripped from her pussy and her nipples ached for a hard touch. Her sudden arousal sent flames of need burning through her body. She nearly screamed for the orgasm that seemed just out of reach. What was happening to her? How could simple words nearly send her into an orgasmic frenzy?

Before she could form a protest or a question, he pulled her to her feet and only his arm around her waist kept her standing against the exhaustion and confusion that beat at her.

Holding her close against his broad chest, his heated eyes met hers. "Breathe through the binding."

Her head sank under the pressure that tightened every muscle in her body. She moaned as her forehead touched his chest, instinctively seeking his help.

"Breathe through the binding," he said again, moving his hand to her face. And with his movement, she felt the tension ease and begin to seep away.

Illogically, she sobbed as the pressure eased rather than tipping her over the peak. Eyes closed, Kytar's muscles hard under her cheek, she struggled to regain control of her body. Finally, she whispered, "What happened?"

She felt Kytar's chuckle, deep in his chest. "We've linked and you are officially my companion."

"No…" she moaned.

"Oh yes, little one. The words are not just words. The words are magic, carrying the weight of thousands and thousands of years. Your response to the binding linked us, no matter how much you might wish to deny it. Welcome to Darinth."

Chapter Four

ℬ

Exhausted by her long wait in the arrival center, Marissa didn't resist when Kytar freed her hands and led her outside. The words he'd recited beat in her mind and oozed down into her very bones. Lost inside herself, it took her a moment to make sense of the scene that greeted her.

Despite the early hour, naked and half-naked women filled the street. Some bound and collared. Some leashed to a man. Horrified, she stepped back, right into Kytar's arms.

She tried to turn and reenter the building but he held her close, circling an arm around her waist, trapping her arms by her side. The hard line of his body pressed against her back. Placing a hand under her chin, he forced her head up. Lowering his head to hers, he whispered in her ear. "This is Darinth. These customs are acceptable. You needn't be frightened."

"Let me go. Please let me go."

"Look at the women. Look at their faces. Do they seem unhappy?"

His words shivered down her back. His firm hand under her chin allowed no escape from the scene before her. All the women, even the ones bound and leashed, smiled and seemed content. Some even openly laughed up at the men who accompanied them.

Marissa refused to accept that a woman could be happy in such a situation. "They just don't know any better. You've brainwashed them!"

"Or is it you who has been brainwashed? Taught to ignore your sexuality. Taught to ignore your needs. Taught you must be independent and live your life alone. Misled by abstract concepts of equality. Tell me, do you feel equal now?"

His powerful torso scorched her back. His seductive whisper rippled through her. She longed to sag, to lean on his strength. She resisted his allure and tried once more, "My father..."

"Do you really think he doesn't know about this?"

Marissa's stomach clenched, nauseated by his words. "What do you mean?"

Ignoring her question, he moved in front of her. "Don't fight me, little one. Otherwise, I'll collar you here and now."

Marissa arched her head to look up at him, trembling so hard that only his arm around her waist kept her upright. "Collar?"

"Collaring is a private act, not something to be done on a public street," he continued, moving a hand to the neck of her shirt. With a quick downward motion, he ripped her shirt apart.

Marissa gasped, stunned by his physicality. Used to gentle and considerate men, she'd never considered just how strong a male could be and how helpless she'd be before a man who didn't hesitate to use his strength. Worse, her heart pounded as she responded to his decisive action. She'd never imagined that unrestrained masculine strength might be an aphrodisiac. What happened to her preference for more civilized customs?

But an embarrassing thrill of desire pooled in her pelvis. How could she respond to such brutal treatment?

He smiled as he finished stripping off her shirt and bra. Her cheeks flamed and she cringed, trying to hide her body from his gaze. He pulled her straight and ran his hand over her body.

When he paused over a breast, she held her breath, watching as her nipples reached for his touch.

"You're beautiful," he murmured, fingers grazing her nipples.

She tried to swallow past the lump in her throat, but an arrow of arousal had her gasping for air as her knees buckled.

Her shuddering seemed to have its own life. "What's happening?"

He chuckled. "Hasn't any man ever aroused you?"

"I'm not aroused!"

"No?" He worked a finger down the waistband of her slacks and slid a finger into her pussy.

Her thighs clenched.

"You're very wet for someone who's not aroused." He slid in a second finger. Putting pressure on her clit, he started tapping it in a rhythm that forced all her attention to her pelvis.

Ignoring their public position, he held her tight against his broad chest, not letting her squirm as molten heat flooded through her veins. Lost in sensation, she forgot everything except her need.

She moaned as he suddenly pulled his hand free. He chuckled and whispered in her ear, "That was just a small taste of what awaits."

His voice startled her back to awareness. What was happening to her? How could this bastard arouse her? But, he gave her no time to think.

Using her hair as a handle, he pulled her along the street. She stumbled. Her shock and exhaustion, and yes, she admitted, her arousal, made her clumsy and she had trouble staying on her feet. Her checks flamed.

He didn't help her keep her feet, instead, he turned and growled in an amused voice, "Keep up, little one. You don't want me to drag you."

He went another mile and Marissa stumbled along with him. Tears streamed down her face. Sweat trickled between her breasts in the light of the harsh Darinthian sun. Even dawn was hot. Did nothing cool the planet?

Marissa wanted to scream at the people they passed, to scream for help but it was pointless. She was not the only woman dragged along the street. There were many others and men accompanied almost all. Some women were even collared and leashed. At least she didn't have to suffer that indignity.

The nightmare journey finally ended. Marissa shook her head in confusion when she saw the beauty of his yard. Filled with lilacs and lavender, the peaceful scent of the grounds nearly overwhelmed her control. How could he live with such beauty and be so ruthless?

Once through the doorway, Kytar placed his hands on her shoulders and forced her to kneel on the cold marble floor. "Stay there," he ordered as he stepped back, ignoring Marissa's trembling and his need to comfort her. He needed to cool down, to still his raging lust. He could afford a moment to regain his balance.

He'd accomplished his mission of bringing her to his house. She'd left with him, completing the first part of his plan. But his plan hadn't included binding her. He shouldn't go any further. He shouldn't offer her his collar. But, the magic beat at him.

He could feel her arousal feeding his. Looking down at her trembling body, he realized he didn't want to stop. He wasn't certain he could stop. The intensity of their link stunned him. He'd said the claiming words to many other women, but never had the connection locked into place with such strength. No other female had nearly climaxed as the words created the connection. Even worse, he'd nearly been overwhelmed by lust and come close to losing control. Had he done so, Marissa would be dead now. He shuddered at how close it had been and wondered if they'd survive the next linking. No other female had triggered his need like this.

He was rock-hard. He longed to sink his cock deep inside Marissa, to claim her in every way a man could claim a woman. No woman had ever tempted him the way this one did. He longed to subdue her and teach her Darinthian customs. A yearning to complete the ritual flooded him. She would wear his collar.

She deserved his collar. Her bravery combined with her naïveté was irresistible. She was magnificent. If only she realized what an honor he was about to offer.

Marissa huddled on the cold floor. Shivering so hard she could barely stay on her knees, she tried to make sense of her situation. How could she respond to this bastard and where was her father? Why hadn't he shown up? Had he really abandoned her to this man? Marissa tried to still her trembling limbs. Panicking wouldn't help. How could she get free?

And why—why, why, why—why did she still feel an attraction to her captor? Why did she still feel safe with him? He'd proven that he wasn't safe. And what were those words he'd spoken that clenched her insides in an unbreakable grip? Even now she could almost feel him inside. Still trying to sort out her conflicting thoughts, Marissa looked up to see Kytar's eyes glittering down at her. "Do you accept my collar?"

Marissa raised her head. "What…"

He knelt in front of her. He reached out and held her face in his hands. The ball of tension in her gut loosened a little. He kissed her forehead, and then leaned back a little.

She shuddered under his heated gaze.

"On Darinth, the collar is a symbol of protection. If you wear a collar, no man will hurt you. You may call upon any man for help."

"I wouldn't need help if you'd let me go," Marissa protested, fighting the warmth of his hands on her face.

His eyes turned black and his mouth grim. "I tell myself you don't understand our customs. If you did, you would not refuse what I offer."

"You offer slavery. Excuse me, but I'm not interested in being your slave!"

"I offer companionship. You should be honored by my offer."

Before she could respond, he moved a hand between her legs, opening her lower lips. A finger rubbed against her clit, another one teasing her pussy. "You're wet. You respond to me. I know you feel our link. Do you really think you can deny me?" He rocked his hand back and forth. "Do you want me to suck your nipples, little one?"

Marissa's body throbbed and her breath caught in her throat. His words inflamed her and she briefly wondered why she was fighting his touch. Then she remembered what he'd done and where she was. "No! Take your hands off me!"

His black eyes grew colder. He quickly stood, towering over her. "Don't move," he ordered.

Marissa watched him enter a room and briefly tried to stand. She wanted to escape while he was gone, but the grip of whatever he'd done earlier still held her. The tight ball deep inside, created when he said those words, seemed to send out tendrils into hidden places, holding her down. Frightened by her responses and his ruthless actions, she had no choice but to stay on the floor. Besides, where would she go? Apparently, her father had abandoned her to this nightmare.

Lost in confusion and exhaustion, Marissa didn't hear Kytar come back.

He easily lifted her trembling body. Holding her close, he took her to a small room. He sat with her in his lap. His slow strokes comforted and calmed her.

Despite the fire burning in a circular pit, the room was cool. Books lined one wall and buried under a flood of papers stood a desk. No windows brightened the room, the only light came from the fire.

Kytar's arms held her tight as he continued his light caress. Marissa slowly relaxed, leaning against his broad chest. She stared at the fire, mesmerized by the flickering light and his gentle touch. Tension seeped from her muscles. Exhaustion threatened to overwhelm all her defenses.

Kytar bent and kissed her forehead. One hand slipped to her cleft. Gently massaging, he said, "You voluntarily came with me. You voluntarily submitted to me. Now you will accept my collar?"

The words sounded ritualistic, calling to her, whispering for her to say yes, to submit to this man in every way possible. The intensity of her desire frightened Marissa. What was happening to her? How did he control her like this? She didn't understand. But she was in no shape to figure it out.

Marissa tried to swallow the lump in her throat but her mouth was too dry.

Kytar stared down at her and his black eyes penetrated deep into her soul. The kind man from the arrival center was gone. Left in his place was a man used to mastering females. She thrilled, even as she cursed herself for her position.

She bit back a moan. How could she fight his strength and his knowledge of her body? Maybe she could get him talking. "Why…why are you doing this?"

His hand tightened a little. "You felt the magic. Do you think I have a choice?" Not waiting for an answer, he continued in a lower voice, "Your throat looks naked without a collar." A little black leached out of his eyes, replaced by deep chocolate. "The collar means you are mine. Accept my collar," he demanded, "willingly or unwillingly, your choice."

Marissa stared into his black eyes. Unable to break free of a gaze so weighty it felt like fingers deep inside her body, stroking her need. Her head swam as thoughts circled and fought with her body's desire to surrender.

She struggled against her desire and finally managed to scream, "No!" She didn't want to be marked as his. "No! No! No!" she screamed, unable to stop as his words seeped into her bones. "I won't accept it. I won't. I won't."

"Why not? You know you want to say yes."

She stared up at him. How did he know that? He must be mad if he expected her to give in and let him control her.

"You've done well so far." His voice slithered inside, weakening her control. "Will you not even try to follow Darinthian customs?"

She shook her head, fighting off the hysteria that threatened her sanity. She had to stay in control. "Your customs aren't mine."

He tilted his head, searching her face as if she were an interesting specimen. "I've never tried to tame an off-worlder. Your actions anger me. It is not a good thing to anger me." He paused and traced a finger down her face then across her lips.

"Let me go. I don't want to be here."

"Yet you came to Darinth willingly."

"I came to see my father, not to be a slave to any man."

"Companion, not slave and you don't know your father at all," he said slowly.

"What do you mean?"

"Do you really think your father would turn his back on Darinthian customs given his position? He won't. Daughters belong to their fathers until taken by a man. Do you really think your father planned differently?"

Marissa stared at Kytar. His horrifying words echoing deep inside. It couldn't be true! "I don't believe you! He wouldn't do that! He told me I'd be safe."

"As did I. You never asked what the word safe meant, did you?"

Marissa stared at him, eyes wild as she filled with horror.

Kytar continued stroking her cheek. "On Darinth, safe means being the companion of a strong protector. Safe means your protector takes care of all your needs. Safe means never having to please anyone other than your protector. I will keep you safe, even as your father would have. Despite your fears, Darinthian males cherish females. You'll be safer with me than you've ever been before."

"No..." Marissa tried to shout, but the lump in her throat caused her voice to come out in a whisper. "I don't believe you."

"You'll learn. The real question is whether I'll break you before you bend to my will," he murmured almost to himself.

"What do you mean?" She tried to shrug off his finger, but it followed every movement of her head.

"By now a Darinthian woman would be submissive and compliant."

"How boring," Marissa spit out before she could stop herself.

Kytar threw back his head and his laughter boomed over her. "Perhaps you're right. You are a challenge. But your senseless resistance angers me and that is not a good thing. You need to respect my anger and work to satisfy me. You don't understand our world. You have no idea of how easily I could break all your resistance. Do you really think you can defy me?"

The truth of his words frightened Marissa. Kytar's strength thrilled her much as she wanted to deny it. She wanted to rage at him. She wanted to force him to let her go, even as she wanted — no, she longed — to submit to his will and let him take care of her. She could finally be with someone who cared. She never imagined she'd have to fight her own desires as well as his. How could she survive this nightmare?

She closed her eyes as if she could close him out. Exhaustion and shock kept her silent.

The soft touch of Kytar's lips brushed her cheek just before he said, "Will you accept my collar?"

"No..."

"You know I can force your compliance."

Marissa took in a deep breath, steeling herself, she said, "Yes, I know you can force me. You'll have to force me. I won't accept willingly."

She heard his sigh.

"You're tired and in shock. You need to rest and recover your strength. And I have the perfect place for you to do that."

He stood with her still in his arms. His strength amazed her. No man had ever carried her before. She wasn't so thrilled when she saw her new home though. He'd brought her to the cell. Chained her and left her.

* * * * *

Three days later, Kytar tried to shake off the need throbbing through his body. He'd never meant to offer his collar. He'd never meant to keep her beyond an hour or two.

He'd designed his strategy carefully. By capturing Marissa, a female belonging to Davo's clan, Kytar gained power. Marissa's mere presence gave him the advantage he needed. Davo would pay to recover his daughter.

Even now, Kytar's plans weren't in total ruin. He didn't have to go any further, he could still bargain with her. Since she'd refused the collar, the binding hadn't gone too far to reverse. Kytar told himself he should contact Davo and negotiate Marissa's freedom. The smartest action was to stick with his original plan. He should release her to her father's care. Binding Marissa further threatened all his plans.

But even as he reviewed his logical goals, he knew that contacting Davo and freeing Marissa was beyond him. Despite the fact the collaring and binding were not complete, Kytar felt helpless. He couldn't bear the thought of giving Marissa to any other man, even her father. Kytar wondered how her father would react. He might welcome Kytar to the family or he might declare a feud. But even if it meant war, Kytar had no choice. The binding had never possessed Kytar like this before.

He shook his head and poured himself a drink. Many women had asked for his collar. He'd easily refused them, not feeling the need to bind them permanently. Now, here he was offering the honor to an off-worlder who had no idea what it meant. Why did he feel compelled to go so far?

The binding meant power, both symbolic and real. A collar was the equivalent of a wedding ring. Once collared, a woman forever belonged to the man even as he belonged to her. There was no divorce on Darinth.

He'd heard tales of the magic of the binding. He'd heard that the binding would occur unexpectedly and with an undeniable strength. He never really believed the stories until now. He gave a bitter laugh, knowing his tenuous control wouldn't last much longer.

What was there about the woman that made her so different? Was it her independence? Her vulnerability? Her beauty? Yes, her beauty called to him, but he'd known many beautiful women. Whatever the reason, he'd never before faced this raging, nearly uncontrollable need to posses a woman. Her response to the binding was unmistakable. And for the first time, a response echoed deep within, binding him as well as her. He would have her willing compliance.

Her initial refusal hadn't surprised him, but he hadn't expected the blinding rush of rejection her words had caused. He'd nearly lost control and only the knowledge that she was frightened and ignorant of Darinthian customs had stilled his rage.

Marissa didn't know what binding meant. Darinthian customs had an unsavory reputation in the rest of the galaxy. Outsiders didn't understand that magic that was an integral component of sex and companionship on Darinth.

51

He had exercised every ounce of self-restraint not to force her compliance. He couldn't force the binding on her. He knew the truth even if she didn't. If he forced her compliance, the final binding wouldn't work. The magic of the words accepted only truth.

He had her in his house. The collaring would occur regardless of the danger Davo presented. Kytar just needed to be patient and rein in his need to extend his claim in every way possible.

He'd thrown her in the cell for her own protection. He hoped the cell would soften her. Some resistance added spice, but too much fueled his anger. He didn't want to hurt her. He just wanted her submission and he would have it. Today's visit had gone well. She'd nearly climaxed when he'd played with her clit. Her body wanted him, even if her mind wasn't quite convinced. He contemplated the two kisses she owed him.

Marissa didn't know what she faced. Her willingness to leave with him, the first step in companionship, gave him the power to read her emotions. He smiled. She didn't know her own body. She didn't know the power of the binding. She had no idea what to expect and he'd use her ignorance to make her his.

He had to make her his. He needed her. He longed to sink his cock deep inside her warmth. But he wouldn't take her, not yet, not until she'd accepted his collar. He needed to concentrate on gaining her acceptance of his collar so he could finish the common binding ritual. Then he had to deal with Davo. He needed to move just one step at a time.

And the first step required gaining Marissa's complete surrender.

He considered his options, knowing there wasn't a lot she could do to stop him. Strategy had always been one of his strengths and his campaign with Marissa required every bit of his skill, testing him every bit as much as it tested her. He considered one action, then another until finally settling on a plan for his next visit. He chuckled as he realized how he would torment her. It would test all his control as well but she needn't know that.

* * * * *

The next time Kytar visited, he seemed to take the very air she needed to breathe. Was he going to claim his kisses now? His presence, both physical and mental, nearly overwhelmed her defenses as once more she backed against a wall. Knowing she couldn't escape his grasp, but trying anyway.

He held her eyes as he stalked toward her. Placing a hand on the wall to each side of her head, he tilted his head, watching her as he moved forward, using his pelvis to pin her to the wall. Rough stone scraped her back while a warm throbbing beat against the juncture of her legs.

Marissa bit her lip to stop a moan. Stiffening, she met his gaze even though her knees weakened.

Kytar leaned down and gently kissed her. Stepping back, he smiled. "That's one kiss."

Confused by his behavior her knees threatened to give out. Her breathing ragged, she'd expected more, not the chaste kiss he'd just bestowed.

"If you are needy, accept the final binding."

She shook her head unable to speak through the fear and need clawing in her abdomen.

"Why do you keep fighting, little one? I've no desire to break you. You must know by now how easily that could be accomplished."

She blinked, trying to clear moisture from her eyes, but stayed silent.

"You are helpless. You are at my mercy. I can arouse you to the point where you will say anything, do anything to have your needs met. Is that what you want, do you want me to arouse you to the point of mindless surrender? Is that why you still fight?"

"No! Let me go!"

"Do you really want me to set you free before I've satisfied your needs?"

"I won't be your slave!"

"Companion, not slave," he replied. "I know your customs are different. Surrender and I'll show you there is nothing to fear and much to gain by being my companion."

"But Darinthians subjugate females. I won't let any man control me," she said, remembering her stepfather's brutality.

Kytar sighed. "But I am stronger both physically and mentally. I do control you whether you wish to admit that fact or not. It's not such a bad thing, little one. I will take good care of you."

Marissa shook her head. "No."

Kytar's eyes hardened. "You know nothing of our customs. You reject them without understanding. You will surrender to me. Surrender and you'll know satisfaction beyond anything you've ever imagined."

"You'll take me whether I surrender or not. So what difference does it make?"

"I know our customs are different. The rest of the galaxy has painted us as evil dominators of women. That is not an accurate portrayal of our relationships. I will not take you without your consent. Do you surrender?"

She shook her head.

"Why would you deny yourself the opportunity of uniting your mind and body? The union between linked couples creates an amazing arousal and satisfaction. Would you like a demonstration?"

Tears filled her eyes. How could she fight this man? The screams of her body made thinking difficult.

"I control you, little one. There is only one more step for the common binding ritual. Take it," he whispered.

She closed her eyes, wishing she could close him out as easily. Everything about him called to her senses. She couldn't just submit to him, could she?

She forced her eyes open as his cedar scent engulfed her, carrying her away to a distant forest. His tight sleeveless shirt and pants clearly revealed rippling muscles and the length of his hard cock. He wanted her, of that, she was certain. And he was not a small man.

Her thighs clenched. Did she want him to force his way inside her? Marissa was petite, she wouldn't be able to take him easily, but she was anxious to try. Why not just have sex? Why did he demand her surrender?

Kytar stood motionless, a hand span away.

Marissa wanted to move away from him. His close presence confused her but if she moved from the wall, she wouldn't be able to stand. His chaste kiss had weakened her more than hours of foreplay and her knees shook like jelly. She should surrender. He wouldn't stop until she did. How much longer did she really think she could hold out in the face of his implacable demands?

"If…if I surrender…" she struggled to force the words past her tight throat.

"If you surrender I will protect you."

"What…what does that mean?"

"It means you are mine and I will protect you."

"No! No man owns me!"

"Yes, little one. I do own you much as you own me. The link goes both ways. You will accept my collar and the binding." His face was serious. "Your suffering hurts me. Let me soothe you. Let me caress you. I guarantee our joining will be unlike anything you've ever experienced."

His soft voice seemed to seep inside her. His heated gaze melted her frozen bones. Would it be so bad to surrender? He'd gain her compliance eventually. They both knew that. The only question would be how broken she'd be by the time she said yes. Did she really want to push him into forcing her compliance?

He stood over her simply watching her struggle, waiting for her answer.

Marissa trembled, struggling with conflicting desires. She sagged, teeth chattering, confused by the violence of her response, she remained silent.

Chapter Five

❧

"Marissa, you suffer needlessly. Surrender to my will," Kytar said, pulling her into a hug. "Let me take care of you, little one."

His arms surrounded her in a cocoon of strength and warmth. How could she feel safe when he was the one causing all her turmoil? She tried to pull back, but he sat on the floor, pulling her into his lap.

She could feel his cock throbbing underneath her buttocks. Despite her fear, her pussy echoed his throbbing. She wanted him buried deep inside. She wanted to feel his power over her. She wanted everything the women in the vids had experienced. Her breasts ached for his touch, but he didn't try to caress her.

Instead, he enveloped her, holding her close, pulled tight against his rock-hard body. His warmth seeped into her until the shaking lessened just a little. Her tears flowed freely, unstoppable. She lost her will to fight. She wanted the safety he promised. She wanted his love, as those women had seemed loved. Could she trust him to do that?

The question spurred her anger. Men weren't trustworthy. Hadn't her stepfather taught her that? And she definitely couldn't trust this man. He'd lied to her and tricked her. She ignored the longing in her body and shoved herself out of his arms. Fleeing as far as she could, she screamed, "No!" But she didn't know if she was screaming no to his demands or no to her own body.

Kytar rested his head against the wall. Still sprawled on the floor, he should have looked harmless. Instead, his eyes hardened and brown leached to black. His mouth tightened and after a moment, he stood. Anger radiated from every line of his tight and hard body.

Marissa was in trouble. She longed to flee but there was nowhere to run. Had she pushed him too far? She didn't have time to answer her question.

Blinding speed had him before her before she could even blink. With his hands on her shoulders, his foot swept her to the floor. She landed hard, the breath knocked out of her and before she could recover, he'd pinned her to the floor. All of his weight rested on her, forcing her to take shallow breaths.

He bent his head to her nipple. An arcing need raced through her as his tongue laved her nipple. Wet with desire, she tried to squirm away, but his hips ground her into the floor and she could feel his hard, large length pressing her down. She bit her lip to stop a groan of need, but he continued his relentless assault and when he bit her nipple, her moan escaped.

Raising his head, he said, "A little pain can be good, can't it, little one?" He slid a finger between them, into her dripping pussy, and started tapping her clit. The pressure didn't send her over the peak — it was just enough to drive her crazy.

Her breath hitched. "Take me," she demanded.

"Surrender."

"No! Just take me," she screamed.

He looked down at her.

Marissa could see him struggle as he closed his eyes, breathing deeply.

When he opened his eyes, they'd softened. A little of the black had bled out allowing a touch of brown to return. "You push me too far, Marissa. That is a dangerous thing to do. I never want to cause you pain while I'm angry. Pain, if used at all, is a tool to accentuate your arousal. To turn off your mind and arouse you to heights you never knew existed. Even when used as a punishment it occurs while I am in control. I have never used pain in anger, but you push me too far."

He said the words softly and Marissa had the feeling he said them as much to remind himself and bring himself back under control as he did to warn her.

"Couldn't..." she started before trailing off.

"Couldn't what, little one?"

"Couldn't we just have sex?" The words spewed out in a rush. She was horrified she said them but the words seemed to have a life of their own. Embarrassed by her boldness, she rushed on. "I'm attracted to you. I admit it. We both know you'll have to break me to force my compliance. I don't think either one of us wants that. Why can't we just have sex?"

His eyes cooled. "You insult me by offering such a thing. You insult us both and deny yourself the ultimate pleasure. You don't understand our ways or you would never suggest such a thing."

"Then explain," Marissa cried out. "Tell me what is going on. I don't understand."

With a quick movement, Kytar rolled off her and stood looking down on Marissa. Her naked glory spread before him. He struggled to control his raging desire. Her offer sent sharp shards of nearly irresistible craving through him. No woman had ever challenged his control this way! No woman had ever tried to dismiss the binding. No woman just offered sex. Darinthian women knew better.

Marissa challenged everything he believed, every custom of Darinthian males. He couldn't, he wouldn't accede to her demand for sex. He reminded himself that she didn't know what she asked for, but that didn't still his racing heart and his desire to possess her in every way possible.

He watched her push to her knees. Her movements to cover her nakedness just inflamed Kytar, making him more aware of her body. Her nipples peaking through her hair were sharp points begging to be touched and pinched. He longed to teach her to scream for his touch.

He drew a deep breath, forcing his pounding heart to slow, his raging hard-on was harder to control but he knew he had to control the situation. Maybe if he explained she'd understand the danger of what she demanded. But how could he explain something that every person on Darinth knew? Her world, her customs were so different.

He had to do something though. If another male ever heard her words, she'd be lost, damaged beyond repair. He started slowly, "By our customs there are two common status positions for a female. She is a slave or a companion. Slaves have no rights. The rest of the galaxy believes all our women are slaves."

Marissa started to exclaim. Kytar held up a hand to stop her and continued, "An unaccompanied female is vulnerable to slavery. She won't stay free long. Any male may use her without a binding. Once used by a Darinthian male, without the binding, he is under no obligation to keep her, to help her or to protect her in any way." He drew a deep breath through flaring nostrils, then another, before continuing, "An unaccompanied female has absolutely no rights. Any man can and will use her. After he uses her, he'll likely sell her to a pleasure dome. I'm sure you've heard of our pleasure domes where a man can do anything to a woman. It's where we make the vids we export."

Marissa's eyes widened, remembering the vids she and Shelley had seen.

"In the pleasure domes a man feels like a god. Anything he wants, no matter how painful or dangerous is available. Ignorant foreigners buy the women in the pleasure domes. Those women have no spirit, it has been broken. They submit to many, many men every night. Their backs bleed from the slashing whips of amateurs, men who think that domination is debasement, that a female is a slave. Women in the domes have no rights, no hope and no recourse."

"That's barbaric," Marissa spit out, horrified by the slashing coldness of his words.

"Yes, it is. That's why it is so rare for a Darinthian female to be without a master. To be alone means that no man cares about her enough to protect her. Most of the slaves in the pleasure domes are from off-world. They chose a life of slavery. They are rarely Darinthian women who well know the difference between slavery and companionship. Companions are valued and cherished. I offer you companionship."

"I don't want it."

"You'd prefer slavery? Slavery or companionship, those are your only choices on Darinth. Our women refuse to travel unaccompanied. Yet, you came here alone. You left yourself open and vulnerable. Believe me you should be on your knees thanking me that I accepted you as a companion. I could have used you as slave and turned you over to a pleasure dome."

Marissa's stomach roiled at Kytar's words. "I didn't...I didn't know of your customs, besides my father said I'd be safe in the arrival center."

"Did you feel safe? Didn't you notice how the men in the arrival center looked at you when you were alone? I'd be amazed if you told me no man approached you."

Marissa's eyes widened, remembering the man who'd propositioned her.

"And didn't you notice the men looked at you differently once I'd arrived?"

Marissa gulped. She had noticed that the looks had changed, she just hadn't realized why. "But the arrival center is a safe zone."

"Yes, but they still looked and evaluated and dreamed of luring you out. My presence prevented that. Once I arrived and stood next to you, the other men realized you were protected. Darinthian men respect the females of other men. Simply by standing next to you, I kept you safe from the others."

His relentless words beat into her brain.

"Similarly, on the walk here, my hand in your hair told the other men that we'd started the linking process and that you had submitted to me. So even though your neck was naked, you weren't free game. Thank me for not making you a slave. Thank me for offering you an honorable position."

She couldn't stop the fear and anger that bubbled up and out. "I should thank you for stripping me naked? For hurting and frightening me? For holding me prisoner? For this hateful cell? For kidnapping me?" She sniffed in derision. "Tell me, Kytar, for what particular act should I thank you?"

At her words, Kytar's eyes seemed to burn. His mouth flattened to a grim line. "I tell myself you don't understand our ways but you go too far."

"You took me against my will. You hold me against my will. You want to collar me. I don't want to be here with you."

"How can you just dismiss the magic between us?" Kytar asked, his eyes black and unyielding. Not waiting for an answer, he continued, "When you left the arrival center, you left willingly. You submitted to me. You responded to the binding of the ritual words. Do you now deny it?"

"You forced me to leave. You left me no choice."

"Yet you offer me sex?" He quirked an eyebrow.

"I can't deny I want you," she whispered.

"But you want me because of our link, because of my actions, not despite them. So why do you fight to control my actions now? Don't you fear that would lessen your desire?"

The cold of the floor seemed to seep through Marissa's knees and she fought to remain steady, not to tremble under his ruthless gaze. A scream struggled to escape her throat. She had to get away from this man. Tears filled her eyes as she watched him resume his pacing, as if he was trying to work off his anger.

When he finally stopped and turned back toward her, his eyes held a touch of brown. "The fact I accompanied you and said the binding words means that I promised to take care of your needs, physical, emotional and spiritual, all of your needs."

Marissa didn't want to know any more. He sounded so serious. Much as she wanted to, she couldn't deny the sense of safety that surrounded her when he was near and the lust he generated was agonizing. She wanted him like she'd never wanted a man before. Could she continue denying him? Did she want to?

She needed more information. Not understanding Darinthian customs had allowed Kytar to mislead her. Was he misleading her now? There was only one way to find out. "And if I accept your collar, what does that mean?"

"If you accept my collar, I'll finish the binding. It means I accept my responsibilities until death. I will not renounce the binding. I will not trade you or sell you to another. I will protect you and keep you safe. I will cherish you and meet all your needs."

Marissa stopped breathing, stunned by the effect of his words. If she let him collar her, she'd never be free, why did she want to say yes? Her response made no sense to her. She stalled. She had to think of a way out of this. "You mean like marriage?"

"You may think of it like marriage and the collar as a wedding ring. But there is no divorce on Darinth. Collaring and the completion of the common binding ritual will tie us together forever, until death."

"You don't even know me! Why do you want to go so far? Why can't we just have sex?"

Kytar's eyes bled to black as his mouth tightened. "Once more I tell myself that you don't know what you ask, you don't know our customs. But that fact doesn't lessen my anger, little one. You push me too far. You need to be careful."

"What am I asking? Tell me then, so I'll know!" Fists clenched at her side, her breaths ragged, she waited for his answer.

"Despite our reputations, Darinthians value monogamy and chastity."

"But..."

He waved a hand, "Yes, I know our reputation. Others in the galaxy have perverted our sexual customs into something vile because they don't understand the magic of the binding or the way we use pain and no Darinthian will speak of it to outsiders. And yes, I know you've had sex. But you've never sex with a Darinthian."

She frowned in confusion.

"Your actual physical state doesn't matter. Remember I called you virgin to our planet?" He quirked an eyebrow in question and waited for her nod before continuing. "By publicly declaring you a virgin to our ways and by treating you as such, I declared you chaste. I chose to claim you and to protect you, rather than just use you."

"Maybe you should just let me go, since I'm damaged goods."

"You will only be damaged goods if I accept your offer to fuck you," he shot back. "I've offered you an honorable position on Darinth. To counter, with the offer of a fuck, is an insult to both of us."

"You...you can't...you can't mean that sex —"

"Darinthian customs go far beyond sex. Sex is a meaningless physical act of momentary gratification. Physicality, without mental and spiritual binding, is shunned by most Darinthians."

"You make it sound like a religion."

A brief smile twisted Kytar's lips. "It is sacred. Magic is involved, as you've already felt. Power rises as the binding progresses."

"You mean...you mean you...you gain power by putting a collar me?" she finished in a rush.

Kytar smiled. "By finalizing our link we both gain power. Even now, you can feel my touch brushing your mind and the threads that link us, can't you? If we have sex now, before the common binding is completed it means neither of us gain more power. I've worked too hard to trade power for a quick fuck."

"You mean if you have sex with me now it will hurt your power base?" Marissa asked, disgusted by the fact she might simply be a pawn in a power game.

"Yes, sex means I'd gain no more power but neither would you. If I agreed to your request, you'd remain mastered. I could never collar you but I could sell or trade you. Is that what you want? Do you want me to trade you to another?"

Marissa's heart stuttered. While Kytar terrified her, at least she was attracted to him. She remembered the other men at the arrival center and the men in the street. No, she didn't want him trade her to another. Still struggling to understand she asked, "But, sex would protect me from collaring?"

Kytar sighed. "I would not be able to collar you, but, you are mistaken if you believe escaping me means you'll be free. Another man could still claim you. You'll never be free again. Your only choice is your status. Whether you admit it or not, you want my collar. My strength arouses you or you wouldn't have offered sex. You want to feel me deep inside you. You really don't want to be free."

"But I don't want to be trapped here forever!"

"Don't you?" He quirked an eyebrow in question. "Was your life so good before?" He didn't wait for an answer before saying, "You belong with me. I will keep you safe. I will protect you." He lowered his voice. "You ache with a need only I can satisfy. And I will satisfy you, but not until you are mine and the common binding ritual is completed."

He stopped pacing and frowned at her. "Enough of the games, little one. You are on my world. You will accept our customs. I hold your life and your happiness in my hands. I know you don't understand so I've made many allowances for you. I've tried to explain how tenuous your position is, but I can't control my anger much longer. It's time for you to surrender to the power of the magic that links us."

Marissa gazed up at him, meeting the hard black coldness of his eyes. Every line of his body was tight. His mouth flattened in a grim line. Not a hint of softness marred his face.

Pushing him further was dangerous. Furious with herself, she admitted that she wanted him. His cold words hadn't cooled her ardor. How could she even consider his proposal? It was barbaric, but it was also wildly arousing. No man had ever cared enough about her to delay his own gratification, boldly claiming her as his. Or was his concern for her just a side effect of his desire for power? That thought sent a stinging shard of disappointment through her.

Her mind circled while he waited. His reasoning really didn't matter, did it? Surrendered or be sold, that was her only choice. Was he lying about everything? She didn't think so. She was convinced he'd sell her if she refused him. She didn't dare take the chance. It was just a collar, no matter what he claimed it symbolized. It was just a piece of jewelry she could always remove, she told herself.

Chapter Six

ℬ

Despite the fact Marissa refused to accept the symbolism of the collar, fear weighed down her head as she faced her decision. She didn't want to stay in this cell and she knew Kytar would keep her here until she surrendered. And he'd help that surrender by driving her into frenzied need. She couldn't fight him anymore. Tears filled her eyes. She shook so much she had trouble staying upright. "I..." her voice trailed off, she didn't know how to force the words past the lump in her throat.

Though a film of moisture, she saw Kytar kneel in front of her. His hand under her chin was gentle as he raised her head. "Will you accept my collar?"

She took a ragged breath, almost feeling him deep in her head, comforting and encouraging her. She nodded.

"I need the words," he said, his voice gentle.

"I..." She closed her eyes and swallowed hard, trying to get rid of the choking tightness in her throat.

His hand released her chin and grazed her nipples, sending a flare of heat into her pelvis before moving both hands to cup her face. Her tension eased. Opening her eyes, she noticed his eyes were brown again, warm and inviting, obviously concerned.

"You're a strong woman. You can say it. You can handle it. I will keep you safe." He waited until she nodded then said, "You voluntarily came with me. You voluntarily submitted to me. Now will you accept my collar?"

The words seemed to resonate deep inside Marissa, giving her strength, lessening her fears, dissolving the lump in her throat. "I accept…" She took a deep breath, straightening her spine. She met his eyes and said, "I accept your collar."

He smiled at her and lightly brushed her lips with a finger. "I welcomed your presence. I accepted your submission. Now I will give you my collar and mark you as mine. Let us finish the common binding."

The words thrummed throughout her body, causing her to shake so that she could barely place her hand in the one he held out for her. She couldn't stand without his help. Help he gave freely as he pulled her up and circled an arm around her waist, supporting her as he led her out of the cell.

Why did she feel safe and protected? For the first time in her life, she wasn't alone in the galaxy. She'd always be with Kytar. Yet he was going to place a vile collar on her neck. There was no escape, so why did she trust him? Hadn't her stepfather's actions taught her anything? She longed to pull away to protest again that this wasn't right, but then why did it feel right? Why did she feel such a connection with this stranger?

The strength of his arms kept her upright as he led her down a hallway. How had he overwhelmed all her beliefs about herself? Was she really so weak? Had she always wanted a protector? All her beliefs about equality flew away in the face of his strength.

Kytar slanted a glance down. He could feel Marissa's tremors. She was on the edge. If he pushed her any more, she might break. He didn't want her broken. Her spirit called to him. He'd never lusted after a woman like this. Her strength delighted him.

Only her ignorance of Darinthian customs had allowed him to get this far. Until he finished the binding, she could have demanded to see her father. If she'd made the formal request, he would have had to accede, but she didn't know that. Now, it didn't matter. The ritual would soon be complete, binding both of them. One more step then she would belong to him, whether she liked it or not.

At the entrance to the room with the fire, she tried to shrink back.

"I don't think I can do this," her words rushed out in a breathless voice as if fleeing from his intent.

He held her tight, preventing any escape. "Shhh, little one, you make this harder than it has to be."

Her eyes wide and filled with tears, part of him wanted to abandon his plans, but he strengthened his resolve. He had to bind her. The magic gave him no choice. Once he completed the common binding, she would truly be his. Then she could never escape.

The links between them tightened in anticipation, causing her to sag in his arms, trembling so hard she could no longer stand. He picked her up and strode into the room. Gently placing her on the sofa, he lifted her hair and placed a pillow under her head, leaving the long line of her throat exposed. His breath caught. In the collaring position, she was incredibly beautiful with her neck—white and vulnerable—waiting for his symbol of eternal possession.

He bent and kissed along her neck, feeling her shudders so soft and inviting. His cock raged and he closed his eyes, fighting for control. The intensity of his emotions threatened to overwhelm his restraint. No wonder he'd always heard that he'd know when it was time to take the final step of binding a woman. He'd never experienced magic like this in his other relationships.

He fought to regain control. If he lost control now, he'd lose her. He had to stay strong for both of them. Unlike a Darinthian woman, she couldn't help herself during the binding. She didn't know enough. She didn't understand that the ritual tested him and bound him as well as every other male on the planet. He'd recorded her acceptance, forcing all males to recognize the link and respect it. Collaring her gave

Marissa protection that she didn't understand and believed she didn't need. She'd learn, but not just yet.

Kytar, his hand gently holding her throat, felt Marissa swallow. Her eyes showed her fear as she looked up at him. He placed a hand on either side of her head, sending her a calming energy. "Stay with me. It will be over in just a few moments."

She nodded, taking a deep breath.

He saw her effort to relax and smiled down at her. Stroking from chin to breastbone, her fear and anxiety slowly bled away. Kytar watched in amazement as Marissa stilled, waiting for him to finish the ritual.

He'd heard that the ritual gave him power over the woman's emotions but he hadn't believed that any woman, especially not this woman, could wait so patiently. Her compliance and submissiveness created a raging need to protect her. He took a moment, just a moment, to savor her submission. Not one squirm or twinge marred her acceptance. All her energy and fire waited for him. He longed to spend another hour enjoying his feelings but it wasn't fair to Marissa to keep her waiting.

He took in a deep breath and pulled the collar out of his pocket. Threading it under her neck, he pulled it snug and he started the ritual.

"I claim you as mine."

Marissa moaned, her lips parted, inviting entry.

He forced the invitation and her moans out of his head. He had to complete the ritual before he could help her. In a strong voice he continued, "I claim you as mine. You are my companion. I own your body. I own your mind. I own your spirit. I claim you as mine."

Something seemed to break deep inside Marissa as she heard the words over the snick of the collar closing around her throat. She screamed as his ownership tightened every muscle in her body, even her bones vibrated with need. She bowed off the sofa, unable to breathe through the raging ball of fire that engulfed her body. She screamed for release as her body soared toward a peak. Through the pain of arousal, Kytar entered her head.

"Marissa, hear me. The pain is receding, soon it will be gone."

The words seemed to echo in her head, just out of reach. She fought to reach the peak, to surge over and release the incredible tightness that gripped her body. Kytar blocked her path to satisfaction and she screamed, "Let me come."

"No! Breathe through the binding. Don't surrender to your satisfaction or we're both lost. Breathe through the binding," he ordered, his hands firmly gripping her face, stopping her surging motion.

Marissa felt her peak move fractionally away from her, she moaned in frustration. As Kytar repeated, "Breathe through the binding otherwise we are both lost."

She wondered what he meant, but she couldn't find the will or the focus to ask. Centered deep inside on the tight ball that was growing, thought was beyond her. And as the ball grew, more tendrils wound through every internal crevice until she was certain Kytar filled her entirety and she knew with a growing certainty that she'd never escape him now. She'd never be alone again. She couldn't deny the magic between them any longer. The collar was not just a piece of jewelry.

Her arousal seeped away and she moaned in disappointment and frustration. Why hadn't he let her come?

She hadn't realized she'd asked the question aloud, but he answered.

As if from a great distance, Marissa heard the words, "The ritual is a test of our control. Had you come during the ritual we would have both died. But you were strong and we survived." He kissed her forehead. "We are bound now."

71

Kytar sat beside her and pulled her up into his arms. His hands stroked her face and neck, creating heat in their wake. Leaning forward, he brushed her lips with his.

Closing her eyes, she cuddled in his strong arms, wondering why she'd ever been afraid, wondering why she wasn't afraid now.

Kytar continued softly stroking her cheek. Smiling, he said, "There is magic here on Darinth, whether you admit it or not. Could I have cut off your questions and your protests so easily otherwise? Could I have stilled your fears or your need without magic? And I know the strength of the link between us."

Her eyes widened. Her mind screamed that he'd victimized her, even while she wanted to surrender to his strength. His collar had triggered something deep within. She finally belonged. She wasn't alone anymore.

"By accepting my collar, you completed your part of the ritual. By collaring you and reciting the words, I completed my part. You are bound to me by magic."

Marissa tried to clear the confused tangle in her mind. She shook her head, still bewildered by her position. She should be angry. She should hate this man but all she felt was a soft contentment and if she was honest, a raging emptiness that demanded fulfillment. She couldn't stop the question that escaped. "Can we have sex now?"

He chuckled. "Are you feeling needy, little one?"

Marissa closed her eyes, cheeks flaming with embarrassment. Desire lurked just under the surface, waiting to explode at his touch. How could she want this man? He challenged everything she understood about her sexuality. Before she could speak, he placed a finger on her mouth, tracing her lips.

"I'd like nothing better than to consummate our union. But I feel your exhaustion. The past week has been difficult for you. And the binding was more difficult than you realize. You need to rest before we proceed. Sleep now."

Marissa's body complied with his command. Though she tried to fight and demand satisfaction, sleep overwhelmed her and pulled her under.

* * * * *

Marissa awoke in a dim bedchamber. She groaned as memories flooded back. She wasn't surprised she was naked under the sheet. At least she was out of the cell. She slowly moved to a sitting position and swallowing, felt the collar encircling her throat. She reached up. Cool metal met her fingers. She sought a catch, but found no seam, no clue as to how the collar came off. Panic threatened to choke her but before she could surrender, an older man entered the room.

Marissa quickly yanked the sheet higher. She didn't recognize him until he moved closer and sat down on the edge of the bed. She started.

"Father..." Marissa whispered.

He looked at her for a moment before saying, "You have your mother's eyes. I saw them on the comm, but to see them in reality is a wonderful thing."

"Why did you abandon me?"

He shook his head. "I promised you safety. I did not willingly abandon you."

"Then..."

"Kytar misled you. I've seen the vids. I know why you left the arrival center with him but..." He shrugged.

"He lied to me? About you, he lied?"

"He never lied—he merely let you make certain assumptions."

"But you can get me out of here?"

"It is far too late for that, I'm afraid."

"What do you mean?"

He pointed toward her neck, "You've accepted Kytar's collar. You belong with him now. That's the only reason he let me see you. He knows there is nothing I can do."

Marissa's stomach sank. She longed to scream in frustration but held herself rigid. "I don't understand."

"Yes, Kytar counted on that."

"Please, please, please explain. I feel like I'm going mad and I'm frightened. I don't understand."

Her father sighed and turned his head away from her searching gaze. His shoulders sagged.

"Father?"

Drawing in a deep breath, he turned to squarely face her. "I told you there were reasons I couldn't leave the planet."

Marissa nodded, silently encouraging him to continue.

"I miscalculated. I thought you were safe from my enemies. I never once considered you'd become a pawn before you officially arrived on the planet or I never would have invited you to Darinth."

"Pawn?"

"I received a message that you'd been delayed." He shook his head. "I should have checked the flight. I should have foreseen..."

Marissa frowned, waiting for him to continue.

"The message said you'd been delayed. I assumed you were taking a later flight and you'd send me updated information. I didn't check. I should have checked."

"You mean he tricked us?"

He paused a moment then nodded. "It was a brilliant plan and it worked."

"You almost sound proud of him."

"Darinthians admire bold actions—especially when they are successful." Davo shrugged. "What he did was legal and well within our customs. Indeed, his actions have been honorable. He could have treated you very harshly. He could have just used you or sold you to a pleasure dome. You should be grateful to Kytar."

"Grateful? Grateful that he fooled us?"

Davo nodded.

"But he lied! To you, to me, at every point he lied!"

"No, you cannot accuse him of lying. I've seen the vids. Not once did he lie. He let us make assumptions and we didn't question those assumptions."

"I didn't know I had to question every assumption!" Marissa whispered.

Sighing, her father said, "Darinthian customs are different. You came willingly to the planet. You willingly left with Kytar. You accepted his collar. That is the reality of your situation."

"But don't you care?"

"Marissa, he didn't have to offer you the collar and I'm a little stunned that he went so far as to complete the binding with you—an off-worlder. He could have made you a slave and hurt you without any repercussions. He's honored you and for that I'm grateful."

Marissa looked at her father. Horror seeped into her soul. "Are you saying there's nothing you can do?"

"The ritual is the equivalent of marriage in your society."

"Then I want a divorce."

A bitter snort of laughter escaped him before he said, "There is no divorce on Darinth. The ritual is magic. Kytar told you that."

"There's no such thing as magic. I don't believe in magic."

"Surely you felt it? Denying its power won't make it go away."

"Then there's nothing..." Marissa gulped trying to swallow past the collar on her neck. "There's no way I can be free?"

Her father frowned. "Why would you want to be free? Kytar is your mate—your other half—otherwise the ritual would not have worked. He will satisfy you in ways you never dreamed possible. I know our customs are strange. But please, give yourself a chance to learn them before you reject them." He paused a moment then smiled. "You might even find you like them."

"I won't be his slave," Marissa spit out.

"You're an honored companion! Don't you dare devalue that status by calling yourself a slave! Kytar could have made you a slave and he didn't."

Stunned by his anger, she moaned, "Why did my mother tell me to come here?"

Her father grimaced as if in pain. "She would have had a place of honor had she stayed."

"Then why didn't she stay?" Marissa asked, caught by his sad tone. "She told me how much she loved you. Why didn't she stay? Why did she accept my stepfather's cruelty? Why did she accept his beatings? He was...he was so vicious..."

Marissa's father stared at her. "Perhaps she found she missed Darinth. Perhaps she sought a substitute."

"You mean she wanted the beatings? How could any woman want that?"

He chuckled. "No woman wants a beating fueled by anger. Punishment done with love and consideration is something else. Every woman wants a strong man." He saw her startled face. "You don't understand our customs. Neither did your mother. At least not while she was here," he said, his voice hardening with emotion. "It is long in the past. Did she say why you should come here?"

"My mother told me to find you," Marissa said, hoping the answer would still his questions.

"And you did, although not the way either of us intended." He smiled ruefully as he shook his head. "Did she say anything else?"

Marissa hesitated. But what difference did it make if he knew? "She said I'd find freedom here." A bitter laugh escaped. "I guess her memories were flawed."

Her father stared at Marissa. She could see his shock but didn't understand it. His eyes shimmered with moisture though he quickly blinked to clear them.

When next he spoke, his voice was barely audible. "You don't understand our customs or you'd know what your mother meant. It gladdens my heart to hear her words. She's given me a priceless apology for her fear."

Marissa just stared at him, confused and angered by his words. He was right she didn't understand. Something about the words had affected him though because he straightened his shoulders. Whatever she'd said had strengthened his determination. But exploring her words gave her no clue and before she could untangle her confusion, he spoke again.

"You want to stay with Kytar whether your mind will admit it or not. And you will stay with him. There is nothing I can do to rescue you."

He paused a moment and Marissa made a small sound to protest, but he held up a hand to stop her. "Stop fighting him. Forget your upbringing. Forget your customs. You are on Darinth now. Stop fighting our ways. Stop fighting yourself. Surrender. Let Kytar lead you and he will take you to peaks you never knew existed. You are bound to him whether you like it or not." He chuckled. "Although I think Kytar will make certain you like it. Perhaps I should have pushed your mother more. It is obvious now, that Kytar's disregard for your customs has accomplished far more than my consideration ever did."

Marissa's stomach sank with his every word. He wasn't going to help her. He wasn't going to free her from Kytar's grasp and that fact froze her mind. Her father's words seemed distant and irrelevant in the face of Kytar's authority. She shuddered as the realization and finality of her position hit with a force that left her stunned.

"I want to be free," Marissa choked out in a whisper. "How can I gain my freedom?"

Davo started as if she'd struck him. "Don't ask that question!"

"Why? Is there a way? How? How?"

Davo frowned. "Marissa, just accept—"

"No! No, I won't accept being his slave."

"Companion, Marissa. He hasn't made you a slave. He's offered you an honorable position."

"No! I don't see the difference between slavery and companionship on Darinth. I won't accept it. Tell me how to get out of this position. How can I gain my freedom?" she demanded.

Davo frowned. "Haven't you already consummated the binding?"

Marissa shook her head.

Davo remained silent so long, Marissa feared he wasn't going to speak but he surprised her by slowly saying, "There is only one way…"

"What? Tell me."

Shaking his head. "No, it is too dangerous. You don't know what you ask for."

"Father, I want to get away from Kytar. How can I gain my freedom?"

His jaw clenched. "The challenge ritual…"

"Tell me."

"The ritual is dangerous for both of you. You do not want to ask for it."

"I couldn't be in a worse position than I am now."

"Oh yes, you could. He'll have two weeks to train you."

"Train me?"

"Yes, he's allowed to fight your challenge."

Marissa gulped but couldn't stop her demand. "Tell me everything."

"If you formally ask for the challenge ritual, he's not allowed to have intercourse with you. But he will have two weeks to do anything else he wants. Anything. Despite our reputation in the galaxy, Darinthian males typically control themselves. During training, there are no such safeguards for a woman. If you demand the ritual, it means that Kytar can do anything he feels will consolidate your binding. You couldn't deny him the collar and he only had you for a short time. Do you really think you can survive two weeks of his attentions and then still say no to him?"

Ignoring his question, Marissa asked, "But if I ask for this ritual, he has to honor my request? What happens during the ritual? What do I have to do to gain my freedom?"

"Marissa, you won't be able to fight him."

"Let me worry about that. Just tell me," she demanded, tired of not understanding Darinthian customs.

"The ritual hasn't been used in my lifetime. I've never seen one but I have seen vids…"

"Tell me."

He sighed. "The challenge ritual is a test of your link with Kytar. He has to demonstrate his control over your sexual responses in a very public venue."

"Why is everything sex on this planet?" she asked, exasperated by his response. Not expecting an answer, she asked another question. "So if he doesn't control me?"

"Then your bonds are broken."

Traitorous pictures rippled through her mind. If she were honest with herself, she wanted — no, she longed — to surrender to Kytar's strength. Davo was right. She hadn't been able to fight Kytar's demand that she accept the collar. How did she think she could fight his training? She longed to feel his cock buried deeply within her, filling her. She wanted his mouth on her nipples, sucking and yes, even biting them. Maybe she should just give in and forget this challenge thing.

Then an image of her mother cringing before her stepfather flooded her mind. She saw her mother's bruised face. She saw her mother curled in a corner while her stepfather whipped her. Marissa wouldn't—she couldn't—just accept her position. She ruthlessly shoved the images of domination aside.

She couldn't just surrender to Kytar. Yes, he'd aroused her, but he'd tricked her. She didn't owe him anything. She had to fight him. She wouldn't give in to him. A few mistakes shouldn't warrant a life sentence on Darinth. She wasn't any man's slave.

"I want the ritual."

"Marissa, there is a penalty for failure. If you don't break Kytar's control of you, if your challenge fails, he'll be able to read your every thought—not just your emotions, like he can now—but every thought in your head. It won't matter if you are a planet or a galaxy away, he'll always be in your head. Not only will he be able to read your mind, he'll be able to control it. He'll be able to stop you from thinking of certain things. He'll be able to make you think other things. The ties that bind become tighter."

Marissa's mouth flattened into a grim line. "If that's the only way to be free of him then I'm willing to take the risk. How do I ask for this ritual?"

"Telling me is enough. If only…"

"If only, what?"

"If only you'd asked to see me. Then I might have been able to do something to free you before it came to this."

"I didn't know…how could I have known that?"

"You believed Kytar's misdirection. You didn't trust me to keep you safe."

"No one's ever kept me safe before, why would I think you would? I want this ritual."

He grimaced, then stood up and kissed her forehead. "I will tell Kytar of your request. He will not be happy." And with that parting statement, he turned and left the bedroom.

Marissa knew Davo was right, Kytar wouldn't be happy. What would he do to her? A writhing mass coiled and tightened deep inside. The situation terrified her. She didn't know how long she stared at the closed door after her father left. She couldn't seem to force her mind to think. She'd been so stupid, believing she could visit Darinth and not be snared in the web of male domination. How could she have been such a fool?

Chapter Seven

ॐ

"She what?" Kytar roared.

"She has requested the challenge ritual."

"How did she even know about it?" His low voice thrummed with anger.

Davo held up a hand. "She asked me the ritual question three times. I had to answer."

"She doesn't even know the ritual questions, much less what they mean!"

"She didn't understand what she agreed to when she let you bind her either," Davo retorted.

"Understanding isn't necessary for the binding to be successful," Kytar bit back. "You endanger her needlessly. Do you really think she can fight me? You had no right—" His grip shattered the glass in his hand.

He looked down at the blood seeping from his hand. "I let you see her before our consummation because I thought there was nothing you could do. Why would you want your daughter to suffer my training?"

"I don't. I tried to talk her out of requesting the ritual. Do you think I want my daughter to go through the hell of training for a test she will fail as long as you remain strong? But…" Davo suddenly sagged, like a balloon leaking air.

He reached for a chair. "You didn't know her mother," he whispered. "I can't bear for Marissa to end up like her. I…I think this step is necessary." Davo bent his head, but continued speaking. "Marissa's mother refused my collar. In anger, not knowing she was pregnant, I sent her away. I thought she'd soon return. I didn't think she could resist the binding. I always thought she'd come back to me. I was wrong. She didn't come back. Marissa told me..." he took a deep breath and straightened. "Marissa told me her mother wed a man who beat her and degraded her."

Davo ignored Kytar's exclamation and continued, "Marissa's mother told her she'd find freedom on Darinth. I can only assume she regretted leaving me."

Davo paused, seeming to collect himself. "I will not have the same happen to Marissa. She feels for you but she can't seem to admit her need. She has her mother's stubbornness. She'll never admit she needs you. And if she doesn't, what type of companionship will you have? She doesn't understand you're not like her stepfather. The magic worked because you're destined for each other. Explaining Darinthian customs seems to have no effect on her. Her stepfather frightened her. She thinks Darinthian customs are the same and she is fixated on a freedom I don't believe she wants. I promised her I'd keep her safe. I believe that your training will bring out her true feelings."

"So you'll make me use methods similar to what she witnessed her stepfather use? How is that going to reassure her? You put us both into hell because you failed with her mother?"

"Your training might be harsh," Davo whispered, "but we both know it will not be like what she witnessed. The bonding will make it different. You know that..." he trailed off as Kytar started pacing.

He stalked around the room as if the movement would dissipate the anger filling him. Davo put him in an untenable position. The ritual was ancient. No one had used it in his lifetime. No Darinthian woman demanded it. They understood its dangers. He frowned. "I will not stint in her training. She will suffer for daring to challenge our bonds."

"I know," Davo said softly. "The challenge will fail and she will learn to trust you. She will be yours. You kidnapped her to gain power and I've just given you the opportunity for more power than even you expected."

"It's not about power, not anymore," Kytar spit back.

Davo laughed. "Oh yes, yes it is. I have faith in you both, even if you don't. You will maintain control. Marissa won't push you over the edge." He paused, then took a deep breath and said, "What can my family do to help?"

Kytar stopped pacing and stared at Davo, startled by his words. Kytar hadn't expected the ritual offer of help, not with Marissa's challenge.

"What can my family do to help?" repeated Davo.

Kytar shrugged. "At this point, there is not much more you can do. I accept your offer and reserve the right to call on you at a later time."

Davo nodded and left.

Kytar stared down at his bleeding hand. He hadn't expected this turn of events. Davo's ritual offer meant that Davo could be trusted, that he really hadn't meant to undermine Kytar's position. And if that were so, maybe Davo's evaluation of his daughter was right. For Marissa's sake, Kytar hoped so because the idea gave him the strength and hope that it might be possible to win her compliance no matter how distasteful the methods of the challenge were.

How ironic that Kytar might have to use barbaric methods to break through the barriers created by the cruelty of her stepfather. Marissa didn't realize how dangerous the challenge was, that both of them would be tested, possibly beyond their endurance. Before he took the step that would put him in danger of becoming like her stepfather though, he'd try to convince Marissa that she didn't want to challenge him.

* * * * *

Asking for the test was right. Kytar had no claim on her. But much as Marissa repeated the refrain, she wasn't convinced. She almost felt him in her mind and somehow she knew he was furious about her demand. How did she know that? Was it magic? Is that why the collar was seamless? Her fingers circled around the collar at her throat but she still didn't find a seam.

She startled out of her tumultuous uncertainty, coming back to her surroundings when her bladder made its presence known. Damn that organ. She'd have never left the arrival center if it hadn't been for its weakness.

She grimaced as she slowly moved off the bed, every movement a throbbing echo of the binding ritual. At least she made some progress. She'd survive this ritual and gain her freedom.

Once on her feet, she swayed a little. Too many shocks, too fast, she thought as she fought off her weakness and made her way to the bathroom to relieve her most pressing need.

Once finished, she splashed water on her face. Looking up, she stared into the mirror. She didn't look any different but hysteria threatened to overwhelm her slender resources. A bubble of laughter escaped as she realized she had someone who cared now. She'd longed for family. She'd longed to belong, but not like this. She should have been more cautious in her wishes.

The bedroom door opened, but she didn't move. Once her nakedness would have sent her scurrying for clothes, but now she didn't care.

Kytar moved into the doorway. Her breath hitched in her throat as she met his eyes in the mirror. His face was serious, with no hint of a smile curving his sensuous lips. Lips she wanted to feel touching her and driving her insane with need. The strength of her lust startled her, forcing her to remember that she didn't want to be here. For a long moment, they simply stared at their mirrored images.

"Little one, you do not want to challenge me."

"Oh yes I do," Marissa spit out. "I want my freedom."

"You won't gain your freedom. Instead, you'll give me even more power over you. Is that what you want?"

"That's only if I fail."

"You will fail, little one. I have two weeks to train you. Do you really think you can hold out against me for that long? Especially when you don't want to hold out?" He leaned back against the doorjamb and crossed his arms.

Marissa eyed his strong muscular forearms, remembering Kytar's strength. Wanting to feel it again, she almost gave in before mentally shaking herself. What was she thinking? She stiffened and said, "I want my freedom."

"Not only will you not gain your freedom, you will hand me total control over your very thoughts. Do you realize what that means?"

Marissa glared at him.

"It means I would no longer have to physically touch you to send you into a mind-shattering orgasm. Simply touching a strand in your mind will cause your body to do everything I command. You really don't want that, do you?"

"That won't happen. I'll be free."

"The ritual is a very public demonstration of my control over you. How will you like submitting to me in front of an audience?"

"I won't submit to you."

"Oh yes. Yes, you will."

His eyes darkened and he moved closer. Placing his hands on her shoulders, he never released her gaze.

Frozen, she watched him use a hand to move her hair away from her neck. Then he lowered his head and gave her a gentle kiss above her collar, sending ripples down her back. "That's two," he whispered into her ear and she couldn't prevent a sharp stab of disappointment. Despite everything, she'd hoped the second kiss would be elsewhere.

He chuckled, as if reading her mind. "You'll not win that easily. Do you have any idea of what I'm going to do to you? I will not fail, little one." His hand moved from her shoulder, down her arm until he could grasp her hand.

"Come along."

"Where?"

Kytar watched the play of emotions across Marissa's face. Anger, fear and desire warred within her. The fear lay just beneath the surface and called to him. He fought off a surge of protectiveness. He longed to pull her into his arms and to comfort her, even as he longed to satisfy them both and consummate their binding. But she'd made that impossible by calling for the challenge ritual.

How could she deny their binding when he could feel her intense arousal every time he came close? She was close to the edge and her awakening called to him, nearly overwhelming him. He exercised every bit of his control to resist her allure. He didn't know how he was going to survive the next two weeks, but he had to. He couldn't afford to fail now.

Davo was right. The fact she could demand the challenge meant she still wasn't his, not totally. Successfully meeting this trial would strengthen their bonds. He'd only seen vids of the challenge rituals. Darinthian woman were rarely assertive enough to call for one. In one vid, the man's power over his companion had been absolute. Her willing acceptance and compliance with his demands had aroused a deep desire within Kytar. He admitted, he wasn't entirely sorry Marissa had challenged him.

If he succeeded—no, when he succeeded—she'd belong to him in unimaginable ways. He wanted to bind her with those unbreakable velvet ties. He ruthlessly shoved aside the memories of the unsuccessful rituals he'd seen, the ones where the women had broken, the ones where the man's control had slipped, lives destroyed before the power of Darinthian magic.

The ritual was not for the faint of heart. It carried its own magic, even more powerful than the binding ritual and far more dangerous. He shoved aside the possibility of failure. He needed her too much to fail. Tightening his grip on her hand, he said, "Come."

"Where?"

"Wherever I say." He hardened his voice into a slashing whip of words. "You are in training now. You do as I say, Marissa. You have no right to question me." All the brown in his eyes fled from his words.

Chapter Eight

ဢ

Kytar led her downstairs. At the door, he paused at a row of leashes. Marissa hadn't noticed them when she'd entered his house, but then she'd been a little distracted. Her heart nearly stopped as she realized he meant to take her out—naked and leashed. She couldn't go out like that! She tried to pull back, but his grip on her hand tightened. Struggling to breathe, Marissa's vision narrowed until she looked down a long tunnel with him at the end.

He slanted a glance down at her.

Eyes wide and wild, she trembled, breasts quivering. He longed to capture them and lick her nipples to full arousal. Lust gripped him and he briefly closed his eyes to shut out the sight of her while he fought for control.

He cursed the bonds between them as he recognized that the magic had trapped him into an untenable situation. All he wanted was to slake their mutual needs, but her challenge meant they'd both have to suffer through the training. Why was she so stubborn? If he gave her an opportunity to escape training, would she take it?

Touching her shimmering curls, he asked, "Why do you deny our binding? Why do you fight the pull between us? I want nothing more than to satisfy our needs. Do you think I want to train you? The ritual is unforgiving and training means I'll do things to you that I'd normally never consider. Don't force me to train you because if you do, I'll hurt you until you comply without question or hesitation. Is that really what you want?"

Marissa's spine stiffened. "Of course not. And if you don't want to do this, why don't you just let me go?"

"I am bound by the magic as are you. Can you honestly tell me you don't feel the link between us?"

He watched Marissa's hips squirm and her thighs tighten. How could she continue to deny her need? "We are fated to be together. Call off the unbinding," he said, voice husky.

"No. No. No. I won't give in to this barbaric custom," she shouted.

Their gazes locked for a long moment until Kytar moved a step closer. "Then you'll do what I say, when I say and how I say," he said as he hooked a finger into her collar. He frowned and pressed his fingers together. A flash of light released a ring and he attached the leash.

She stumbled as he pulled her tight and he hesitated again. She wasn't ready. He pushed her too hard and too fast. He wanted to reassure her and tell her everything would be okay, but he knew it wouldn't be okay as long as she demanded the ritual.

Gritting his teeth, he shoved aside his uncertainty. He only had two weeks. He had to be strong for both of them. But maybe he could give her a little comfort. He stroked a finger down her flaming face until it was under her chin and tilted her head up.

"You have no reason to be embarrassed," he said, using his other hand to pull her even closer, crushing her breasts against his chest. "Public nudity is accepted on Darinth. No one will think it strange that you're naked."

"And leashed? Like a dog?"

"Your collar proves you're mine. The leash is a common custom."

"Not on my world," Marissa spit out.

His eyes hardened to black, frustrated by her continued resistance. "You're not on your world. You're on Darinth now and you've accepted my collar. We are bound, whether you choose to accept that fact or not," he said, pulling on the leash and leading her toward the door.

Marissa reared back.

Kytar stopped and slanted a glance down at her. "Your choice. We go out now or..." he paused until she looked at him, "withdraw your challenge and I won't take you out."

"No. I want to be free."

"You won't gain your freedom," Kytar bit out in exasperation. "You'll learn to accept your place. Maybe seeing other women gracefully submitting to their masters will teach you that women on Darinth don't struggle against their nature."

She clenched her jaw but remained silent.

"You'll see some women walking and other women on their knees. You have a choice of how to accompany me—on your feet or on your knees. Do you understand?"

"Don't do this—"

He gripped her chin, forcing her head back until he met her eyes. "We will go in public. You will go nude. You will proudly walk with me or you'll crawl on your knees. If you insist on the ritual those are your only choices." Kytar turned and walked away.

Marissa tried to pull free, but Kytar tugged on the leash and her neck bowed, causing her to stumble forward. Kytar walked out the door, past the lilacs and into the street, towing her behind. Flashing on the walk from the arrival center, when he'd ruthlessly dragged her home, Marissa knew he wouldn't wait for her. With the leash, he controlled her direction. She had no choice but to go where he went. Marissa frowned. But if she had to be leashed, she didn't have to walk behind him. She hurried a little until she was beside Kytar. He glanced down at her. His lips curled a little, but he didn't comment as she kept pace at his side.

Kytar walked slowly, as if he knew how hard it was for her to stand straight under the weighted gaze of every male Darinthian they met. The looks cast her way were admiring though and as she walked down one street and onto another

Marissa fractionally relaxed. No one was going to jump on her and attack her. Even Kytar couldn't do much in public. The air caressed her breasts, making her realize that she didn't mind her nudity as much as she thought she would, especially when every other woman was naked too.

Marissa saw women walking and women crawling. She couldn't quite understand their expressions of bliss—she wasn't that happy about Kytar leading her around. They seemed happy though, even the ones with lash marks across their buttocks.

She was looking across the street when she heard a male say, "Her gaze is too bold."

Her head flew toward the sound, meeting the harsh stare of a man even taller than Kytar.

Kytar used the leash to stop her forward motion. A quick downward pull put her on her knees.

"Greetings, Talcor."

"Kytar." The man nodded in greeting but never removed his eyes from Marissa.

She quickly looked at the ground. She didn't like the expression she'd seen in Talcor's eyes. He made her feel like an object, not a woman.

Talcor circled them. "Newly collared," Talcor laughed. "I didn't think you'd ever take that step, not after resisting for so long."

Eyes down, barely daring to breathe, trying to withdraw and become invisible, she felt Kytar's shrug. "Some things are worth claiming."

"Her eyes are too bold."

"She's in training."

Talcor moved back a step as if startled by Kytar's words. Then he moved in and knelt in front of Marissa, running his hands over and around her breasts.

When he pinched both nipples hard, she flinched and barely stopped her moan of pain. He reached out and grabbed her chin, forcing her eyes up. Harsh lines framed his mouth. His eyes were a cold blue.

Marissa shivered at the ice she saw in his eyes. Maybe her father had been right. Maybe Kytar had treated her kindly. She knew she never wanted to be in Talcor's hands.

Talcor stood and said, "Davo's daughter."

"Yes."

"She flinches and her responses are far too inhibited."

"She'll learn."

She could feel Talcor's eyes roaming her body, like a cold hand and her nipples tightened. "A delicate problem."

"But a fascinating challenge."

"Worth the risk?"

"I think so."

Talcor nodded. "You know where my allegiances rest. If you need help, you have my willing aid."

"I appreciate your support."

Marissa didn't understand the undercurrent of meaning in the short exchange. Was Kytar going to let Talcor have her? The thought terrified her far beyond any fear she felt of Kytar.

Talcor walked off.

Kytar stood still for a long moment before pulling on her leash. "Stand," he commanded.

She started to walk, but Kytar stopped her. "I didn't tell you to walk."

Startled by the harshness in his voice, Marissa looked up into black icy eyes. "We'll go home now," he stated.

His tone sent a chill of unease down her spine. What had she missed? The exchange with Talcor seemed to have hardened Kytar's resolve. She couldn't feel any sympathy or understanding or comfort from Kytar. It was as if he'd been infused with Talcor's cruelty. Marissa shivered as Kytar led her home, walking too fast for her to keep to his side.

In the entryway, Kytar turned toward her. "Kneel," he commanded and his tone was too harsh to ignore. She looked up at him as she sank to her knees, but he didn't meet her gaze. Instead, he removed her leash and stood, staring down at her for a long time. His mouth flattened in a grim line, he nodded as if he'd reached a decision.

Kytar bent and grabbed her hand. Pulling her to her feet, he led her into the room with the fire. She shuddered, remembering the last time she'd been in this room. Sitting down, he pulled her into his lap and wound his hand through her hair. He used her hair to tug her head back, leaving her neck arched and her collar prominent.

"Whether you like it or not, that's my collar you wear and you wear it voluntarily," he stated. His flat voice sent a thrill of fear through Marissa, even as he bent and used his tongue to trace a line down her neck, sending shivers down her back. Fear warred with arousal and she was unprepared for Kytar's next question.

"What did you think of Talcor?"

Her eyes flew up to meet his. "He frightened me," she responded before thinking.

"You've been frightened since you got here so that is not exactly surprising."

"But..."

He waited for her to continue.

"He seems crueler than you."

"He has a point though. Your eyes are too bold."

Marissa lowered her eyes and stared at the carpet. Kytar seemed strange. What had changed? Was it some dominance thing Talcor had triggered? Marissa held her breath waiting for Kytar's response. She simply didn't understand enough of this world and its customs. Why was he angry? Was he angry with her? What would he do? She didn't have long to wait to find out.

Kytar bent his head and grazed her lips with his. He gently nibbled on her lower lip before moving to deepen the kiss. His tongue demanded entrance. She moaned as she opened for him and her arms crept around his neck, tangling in the hair at his neck. Thought stopped as she fell into the grip of her deepening arousal.

She squirmed, feeling Kytar's cock under her buttocks. She wanted him to feel the same helplessness she did. She wanted him buried deep inside. She needed him and moaned again as his hand played with her nipples, gently pinching and tormenting her, while his tongue possessed her mouth.

She groaned when he broke the kiss. "Don't stop," she demanded her voice husky with need. She tried to pull his head down again, but he grabbed her wrists.

Easily holding her still, he said, "No."

"What do you mean no?" yelled Marissa, fear forgotten as her body throbbed with need.

"Stop! You'll do as I say," Kytar said, his eyes gleaming black as he stared down at her. "Unless you wish to call off the challenge?"

"Damn you! Damn you! I will have my freedom."

"Then I will teach you grace and submission to my will. You can't fight me. You can't make demands. I won't allow your willfulness to continue. It's a danger to us both." Kytar stared down at her. Impossibly, his eyes had deepened even more to icy onyx with no hint of brown. His mouth flattened into a grim line.

She stilled. Had she pushed him too far? Should she call off the ritual? Her heart pounded as fear threaded through her arousal. She moved to get off his lap, but his grip tightened, preventing her escape.

"Your father told me he sent you some vids. What did you like best about them?"

She started at his question, face flaming. She remembered her responses to the vids. Here she was naked in his lap and she'd just begged him to take her, why should the vids embarrass her?

"Tell me, little one. Tell me what you felt," he said in a low and insistent voice.

She shuddered as memories of her responses came back.

He chuckled and a touch of brown bled back into his eyes. "Did you imagine yourself helpless before a man's will? Did you like the way the man focused on his woman's need? Did you hold off on your orgasm or did you find you couldn't wait the way those women did?"

She closed her eyes as his words beat into her. How could he know?

"I know what you felt because you witnessed bindings, not just sex. You demand sex and expect me to comply. Do you really think you'd enjoy commanding me?"

Marissa's breath hitched as she realized that she'd be disappointed if he simply gave in to her.

"Ah, little one, now you're beginning to understand."

She shivered as she looked up at him, knowing she couldn't deny the truth of his words. "What—"

He placed a finger on her lips, stopping her questions. "Your consent is granted under the laws of the challenge. During training I will do things I would normally never consider doing to a companion."

Marissa felt his implacable will deep in her bones. Damn, she didn't know how much more stimulation she could accept before she broke. She wanted to beg him again just to take her. She'd given him control by challenging him, the very thing she swore never to do. The next two weeks loomed endlessly before her. Her stomach sank, could she fight him that long? Then she remembered her stepfather. She had to fight Kytar. She couldn't just give in to him. It was only two weeks. She'd survive.

He picked her up in a tight grip that bordered on painful.

"It is time you learn that I am in charge," he said. Striding toward a door at the far end of the room, he opened it, walked in and set her on her feet.

It took her startled mind a moment to understand what she saw. The room looked like a set from the vids her father sent. There were no windows and the silence in the room told her the walls were soundproofed. Whips, floggers and crops decorated one wall. Another wall held rings at varying heights and chains flowed from the ceiling. A third wall was hidden behind wooden cabinets. Marissa could only image what they contained.

A table with leather restraints and strange attachments stood directly in front of her. She couldn't figure out the attachments, but she knew she wouldn't like their use. She wasn't going to let him use those things on her!

She backed up but ran into Kytar. He grabbed her around her waist. Pinning her arms to her sides, he easily held her with one arm. She tried to kick him, but he ignored her bare feet, tightening his grip until she felt her ribs might crack, he used his other hand to grab her hair. "Stop fighting," he commanded.

Marissa stopped, not because of his command, but because she couldn't do anything else. His hand in her hair kept her head back and up. His arm around her body held her so tight that breathing was a challenge and she feared she'd faint.

Kytar leaned down and licked the line of her neck before nibbling on her ear. His voice, low and seductive, seemed to echo through her body, leaving heat in its wake.

He chuckled. "You cannot fight me, little one," he whispered, rubbing his chin along her neck.

She'd just started to sink into his seduction when he quickly shifted her around and lifted her onto the table. Before she'd realized what was happening, he'd pulled her arms up.

His torso easily held her down while he fastened her wrists over her head.

"No," she moaned, feeling metal bracelets once more. She flashed on her cell and terror overwhelmed her. "Please, don't..."

Kytar ignored her as he pulled a leather band tight across her waist then bands across her thighs and ankles. Finishing his task, he straightened and watched her squirm, trying to free herself.

After a few moments, she stopped and glared at him. "Let me go."

"I offered you an honorable companionship and you threw it back in my face. As my companion, I wouldn't restrain you like this, not without your consent."

"Great! I don't consent to this."

"As long as you are in training for the challenge, you have given your consent for anything I choose to do. Anything."

Marissa caught her breath at his harsh words.

"Think very carefully before you pursue this challenge. I will not let you go. I will train you. Given your continued resistance, I guarantee you won't like my methods because pain will teach you obedience faster than anything else will. Do you really believe you can withstand two weeks under my control? I will have your willing compliance during the ritual. You will not gain your freedom." He took a deep breath, then another before saying, "When I come back, I'll offer you one last chance to withdraw your challenge. Think carefully because if you refuse this time, training will start immediately. And what I've just done is nothing compared to what I will do. There will be no other offers of escape so consider carefully before you pursue this challenge." Turning, he darkened the room and left.

Marissa pulled against her bindings but the leather was firm and unyielding. She couldn't free herself and the unrelenting blackness of the room seemed to press on her chest, making breathing difficult. Sobbing in rage, she finally stilled her body even as her mind raced. How could she get out of this?

She wanted her freedom but the thought of spending two weeks under Kytar's control terrified her. She wouldn't be able to hold out. Part of her didn't want to hold out. His forceful control of her body touched a need she'd never known existed. She'd never felt so alive, every molecule of her body blazing with heat for him. But if she withdrew the challenge, she'd never be free—he'd forever dominate her. She faced two weeks of hell or a lifetime of subservience. Put that way, her choice was clear.

She blinked when Kytar returned and flicked on the lights. Startled, she could feel the effort he made to control himself as he stood over her. She wasn't the only one affected by her challenge, she realized. Could she use his emotions against him?

Her eyes filled with tears. "Let me go, Kytar. You know you don't want to hurt me."

Kytar grimaced as if in pain. He stroked her face, sending calming waves deep into her mind. "I cannot let you go. Custom and magic forged our link. Releasing you means turning my back on my heritage, turning my back on our love. I cannot do that. I will not do that," whispered Kytar. "Marissa, I love you. I want nothing more than to consummate our binding and to cherish you. For the last time, will you abandon your challenge?"

Marissa stared at him in shock. He loved her? She thought all he wanted to do was possess her. But did he love her for herself or as an object that he owned?

"Can't you trust me? I've never hurt a companion without her willing consent. I don't believe you really understand that your challenge is consent for me to do anything I want, anything at all to gain your willing compliance."

Marissa hesitated. Did the fact he loved her, no matter the reason for that love, change anything? He still wanted to dominate her and control her. It was still two weeks versus a lifetime. She slowly shook her head. "I want my freedom."

Kytar jerked as if she'd hit him. "Very well," he said so softly she almost missed it.

He stepped back and examined her supine body.

Marissa fought down the urge to squirm as his hands skimmed over her body. And she gasped when he circled her nipples.

Talcor had left them bruised and the ache of that blended with the ache of need Kytar generated. Her nipples stood out from her chest as if begging for a touch but Kytar ignored them and continued stroking her. After a few moments, the heat pooling in her stomach, combined with the ache of her pussy, caused her mind to shut down.

Kytar looked deep into her eyes and smiled. "Should I leave you like this? Hot and needy?"

"No," she groaned, "please..." Her eyes widened as she realized what she'd said.

Kytar laughed. "Perhaps I'll invite Talcor to satisfy your need?"

"No!" she screamed, horrified by the possibility of his touch. "No. You promised me you'd keep me safe from other men. He hurt me."

"He was merely testing your response to a small pain. You didn't do very well." Kytar continued his light massage, fanning her desire. She almost missed his soft words. "There are only two weeks for training. Pain will teach you obedience faster than any other method. It will turn off your mind and that is what the ritual requires. You must be under my complete control."

Kytar stepped back with a sigh and went to a cabinet in the corner. He opened the door and stood there for a moment, examining the contents. Marissa couldn't see what the cabinet held, but she had the feeling she wouldn't like anything that came out of it.

He reached out and picked something. It was something small, because he held it in his hand and Marissa couldn't see anything. He nodded and pocketed it. He walked back to the table. Using a hand, he brushed her erect nipples, so lightly she moaned. They needed to be touched harder than that.

"Your nipples seem to be begging for something," he said. His voice soft and carefully controlled. "What are they begging for, little one?"

"Touch me, please, touch me."

One finger circled her areola. She tried to move into his touch, but he easily kept his finger off her nipple.

"Please," she begged again. She couldn't seem to stop the word. She needed him.

He ignored her pleading. He used two fingers to caress the base of her nipple, never touching the tip, forcing it to even greater heights.

How could he arouse her so easily? Angry with him for ignoring her needs, she tried to fight off the effects of his actions. He used both hands to caress both her breasts. She wanted to scream but only a moan escaped.

She barely noticed when he reached into his pocket. He bent his head, flicked his tongue over her nipple. Her back arched off the table and she screamed, "More, please, more."

"Gladly," he replied and before she could wonder at his comment, he pulled her nipple out and something cold brushed her breast. Then fiery arrows of pain raced through her nipple, up into her shoulder, ending in a violent pull deep inside her cunt. She arched off the table, trying to move away from the pain, but it followed her every movement and she looked down to see vicious teeth clamped on her nipple.

"No..." she moaned.

Ignoring her protest, he fastened the second clamp and she screamed as her nerve endings flared — both sides in an agony that slowly dulled to a pulling need. Her nipples sent raging heat directly to her pussy. Her body twisted as she tried to escape the grip of the clamps.

Kytar just watched her struggles as she learned to breathe again. She'd barely started breathing through the pain and need when he captured both breasts and massaged them. "No man has taught you the bite of the clamps?"

And as more blood flowed to her nipples, she swam in a world of aching demanding want, unable to answer him.

He bent his head and licked each nipple, going from one to the other, mixing signals in her head. Did she feel pain or pleasure? She couldn't quite tell.

He continued torturing her nipples, flicking his tongue over one then the other, winding her tighter. Every time she nearly came, he withdrew until she arched her pelvis, writhing and screaming, "Please, please, please, I can't stand any more."

"You'll take what I give," he said as he proved she could take more.

Her clit expanded as her juices dripped down. She sobbed when he slipped two fingers into her cunt. Tightening her muscles, trying to hold the contact as he slowly moved his fingers in and out. She was so close, when would he send her over the peak?

His hand left her cleft and moved to her breasts. He placed a hand on her forehead. Marissa felt him in her mind, at the edge of her awareness, monitoring her responses for a moment before he created a barrier. His other hand ripped off one clamp then the other, all the while denying her release.

Tormented, she screamed in frustration.

Kytar smiled down at her as she slowly came down from the most intense arousal she'd ever felt. Her body throbbed with unmet need.

"Take me," she demanded.

"Still demanding? That won't do at all," he said as he started the process again.

Marissa lost track of time. She lost track of herself. She knew she begged, she demanded, she pleaded, she asked but nothing seemed to move Kytar as he brought her up so close to release again and again only to stop and leave her frustrated. Every muscle tight, her body humming with mindless desires, he continued to deny her. Until finally, he said, "That's enough for today."

"No!" Marissa screamed as he turned to leave. "Don't leave me like this."

Kytar turned back. "I decide when you can come and I don't want you coming today. You don't deserve that kind of reward. You aren't obedient enough, but you will be." He smiled and left her in darkness.

Chapter Nine

෨

Marissa woke to find herself once more in the bedroom with Kytar at the foot of the bed, leaning against a post, watching her.

"Welcome back. How do you feel?"

Marissa started to reach for the glass of water near the bed but gasped and quickly stopped the motion when her breasts reminded her of their recent abuse.

"Let me," Kytar said.

He picked up the glass then moved her shoulders so he could slide behind her. Marissa's head rested on his chest as he brought the glass to her lips. Then he placed it back on the table. Marissa wasn't prepared when his arms circled her, his hands firmly on her breasts. His fingers moved, recreating his earlier torture.

"No please, they hurt."

"Breathe through the pain," he said.

She rocked her head against his chest and tried to move away.

"Breathe through the pain," he said again.

She tried, but when his fingers tightened on her nipples at the exact point where he'd earlier placed the clamps, she arched back into him, trying to get away. But he didn't let go and her movement simple caused her nipples to pull even more.

"Breathe through the pain."

"No! No! No!" Hysteria and fear overwhelmed her.

Kytar raised his hands off her breasts, holding them out where she could see them. "Calm down," he ordered her. He placed a hand on her forehead and whispered in her ear, "Calm down."

Marissa's fear and hysteria drained away and she regained control of her breathing. "Damn you!"

"Damn yourself. This is a part of your training and we've barely begun. There is so much more." His chest expanded with a deep breath, heating her chilled back. "Can you really tell me you didn't enjoy your earlier arousal?"

"I would have enjoyed it more if you'd let me come," she spit back.

A chuckle rumbled in his chest. "But then you wouldn't have learned anything. Tell me," he bent his head and whispered in her ear, "what did you learn?"

Marissa's face flamed and she grew very still as she remembered how easily he'd controlled her responses. She'd never been so aroused. She wanted to rage at him, to claw out his eyes, to deny that he had any power at all over her.

"What did you learn, little one? And be warned, if you tell me you learned nothing then I'll just have to do it again until you can tell me."

She swallowed hard, feeling his collar tight around her throat. "Why...why was it like that?"

"First, tell me what you learned."

"Pain hurts," she bit out.

His chest rumbled with laughter. "You already knew that. What else did you learn?"

Marissa clenched her jaw. It was bad enough that he'd controlled her responses without admitting it aloud.

He used his fingertips to circle her nipples. "Say it!"

Marissa shivered as he made his intentions clear. She swallowed but couldn't clear the lump in her throat and her voice came out tight and small. "You...you controlled...my body. But not my mind," she had to add.

"What mind? You weren't doing much thinking." He pressed his lips against her temple. "A little pain turns off your mind. It's relatively easy to mix pain and pleasure, to confuse your senses until they blend and you can't tell the difference."

Marissa's breathing hitched at his words. He was serious. He really was going to hurt her. Somehow, she'd never really believed it. She shook her head, stiffening her resolve. Two weeks, that's all she had to survive was two weeks.

"Your nipples are sensitized. They're bruised and tender, but aching for my touch, aren't they? Do you want an orgasm? Do you feel the need? Are you wet?" His hands moved to the sides of her breasts, stroking them as his words stoked a fire in her mind. She held her breath in anticipation of the pain he could cause. Two fingertips reached out gently touching her peaks. "Relax," he commanded.

She gasped as the fingertips started a small circling motion directly on her nipples, lightly, pleasurable arrows shot straight to her pussy. She felt it respond with moisture and need. She leaned her head into his neck as he engulfed her senses in pleasure. Her nipples demanded more pressure, but he didn't intensify the circling motion. Her hips squirmed. More, she had to have more or this peak of need would drive her crazy.

"Say it," he commanded. "Tell me what you need." His words circled in her mind as his fingers circled on her body.

She tried to fight the need, but the lure of the pleasure was too great, "More," she whispered, "touch me harder. I need more."

At first, she thought he hadn't heard her or understood her or that he'd decided to frustrate her yet again. He simply kept circling for a few more moments. Then with a quick motion, when she'd given up hope of satisfaction, he pinched her nipples between his fingers. Whispering, "Come," he twisted her nipples. Waves of pain crashed through all her defenses but it was the resulting orgasm and blessed relief that caused her to arch off the bed. Only his arms kept her safe.

* * * * *

Kytar sipped his drink and wondered whether he'd survive Marissa's training. He couldn't get her out of his head as he remembered yesterday's responses. He ached to ram his cock deep within her. She'd already begged him to do it. Her responses inflamed him to the point where control was difficult, if not impossible. He prided himself on his control, but Marissa was proving just how false that pride was. The challenge ritual was aptly named, he thought with a grimace. But he couldn't afford to lose control. If his control went, he'd lose her.

He looked up as Talcor entered the study.

"Thanks for coming," Kytar said.

"What's the problem? I didn't expect a call so soon."

Kytar tossed back his drink and moved to pour another. "Drink?"

Talcor shook his head.

Kytar sank into a chair. "I used nipple clamps on her yesterday and nearly lost control." He stated in a flat voice, ignoring Talcor's start of surprise. "She's incredibly responsive. She passed out after repeated arousals and climaxed from a simple touch. I'm afraid of what's going to happen when I teach her the lash or breach her ass."

Talcor stared at Kytar for a moment, stunned by his admission. No man on Darinth willingly admitted that a woman made him lose control. He'd never known Kytar to lose control. Shaking off his amazement, he took a deep breath and straightened up. "How can my family help?" Talcor spoke the ritualized phrase.

"I need a guard. Will you watch so I don't go too far?"

Talcor hesitated. To be a guard during the woman's training meant that he would watch Kytar instruct Marissa. Kytar would be free to extend his actions because Talcor would make sure the training did not break the woman. And that Kytar didn't penetrate her. If Kytar lost control, he might die when the bonds broke. Although Darinthian women believed the challenge was a test of the binding, it really tested a male's control.

Talcor's job included stopping Kytar from going too far. Marissa had to enter the ritual unbreached between collaring and the end of the ritual. Talcor had seen vids of training from long ago. There weren't any other living guards. It had been too long since the last unbinding ritual. The women of Darinth willingly submitted before a male got too carried away. This off-worlder wouldn't know enough to submit. She'd keep fighting while Kytar kept escalating.

Talcor could easily see how Kytar might go too far. But if Talcor agreed to guard them, he'd have to maintain his control. Not an easy task given Marissa's beauty and the fact that training called to Talcor's natural inclinations. He didn't have Kytar's aversion to causing a little pain. He liked dominance and control. He liked taming defiant women. The big question was whether or not he could respect the bond between Marissa and Kytar enough to act as guard? The situation would test his control every bit as much as it tested theirs.

Talcor thought about Pella, his current companion. Luckily, she shared his proclivities. But acting as guard would give him a dangerous edge, one she'd never seen before. In the past, she'd always risen to any challenge and even demanded more. He was the one who had pulled back. It had been a long time since he'd pushed her and consequently, their relationship had stagnated. Both knew he'd never offer her a collar. Still, she liked being with him and she definitely liked new games, especially games with an edge. He knew she'd be anxious to help him vent his arousals after his sessions with

Kytar and Marissa. Talcor felt confident that Pella could and would take anything he demanded, that she'd keep his frustration within a manageable range and part of him eagerly anticipated the things he'd do to her and for her. He knew she could reach a new level, he just hadn't been motivated enough to push her before. Now, he had incentive. Grinning in anticipation, he looked up at Kytar and said, "I'm honored you would ask. Of course I will act as guard."

Kytar nodded with a flash of relief.

Talcor's eyes narrowed as he thought about strategy. "I frightened Marissa, didn't I? It was an intoxicating thing. I'm not surprised that this woman challenges your control. But having me as guard means we can use her fear, can't we?"

Kytar grinned at Talcor. "We always did work well together. The first hurdle is that even after a mind-shattering orgasm, she still thinks she doesn't need to submit to my will."

Talcor shrugged. "Are you really surprised by that? She's an off-worlder. She doesn't understand that the binding only works with companions fated to be together. If she were not your other half, you could not have collared her. She denies the magic, doesn't she?"

Kytar nodded and drained his drink. "You're right, she doesn't believe. Not yet, but she will."

* * * * *

Marissa awoke alone in the bedroom. She slowly stretched her sore muscles. All of them were stiff, as if she'd suffered a beating. She'd never imagined arousal and release could be so all encompassing. How could any man control her responses so easily? His methods bordered on torture. She should be furious but she couldn't deny the heavy ache in her pelvis. He aroused her and satisfied her, even if he did wreak havoc with her control or maybe because he did wreak havoc with it. She tried the idea on like a new item of clothing, then discarded it. She was just too confused to sort it out, she thought, walking in the bathroom.

She was in the bathtub, trying to soak out her aches when she heard the bedroom door crash open. Assuming it was Kytar, she screamed when Talcor entered the room.

He laughed as he strode over to her grabbed her arms, easily pulling her up from the tub. She tried to fight but her fists didn't faze him. He simply grabbed both wrists in a large hand. Pulling the thong that held his hair, setting it free, he quickly bound her hands with it. Then he bent and slung her over his shoulder. She tried to squirm off. He smacked her hard, sending a flare of pain through her rump. "Behave yourself or I'll teach you to behave."

She stilled, frightened by his commanding intensity. Where was Kytar? Where was Talcor taking her? She cautiously lifted her head, trying to see they were going. Talcor ignored her small motion. But raising her head pushed her pelvis deeper into his shoulder. Her cunt ached in emptiness. She wanted it filled, but not by this man. Where was Kytar?

Before her anxiety could rise even more, Talcor strode into the room she'd nicknamed the dungeon. A quick motion tumbled her onto the table. He bound her arms before she'd recovered her breath. Moving down the table, he grabbed her ankles and spread her legs, binding them far apart. He trailed a hand up her leg and past her gaping pussy. He paused there a moment, tormenting Marissa with images of him violently entering her but he continued upward, finally harshly rubbing a hand over her nipples that were still bruised from yesterday.

"Beautiful," he said but she wasn't sure if he meant her breasts or the bruises that blossomed on them.

He smiled down at her and a chill of fear took the question out of her throat. He trailed a finger down the side of her face, pausing briefly at the corner of her lips. "Patience," he said, then he turned and plunged the room into darkness as he left.

Marissa's heart threatened to pound out of her chest. Where was Kytar? Didn't he say he'd protect her? Where was he? She struggled with the bindings but couldn't loosen them at all. She lay on the table like a virgin sacrifice with her legs spread, vulnerable and helpless. Her skin chilled as time passed. Where was Kytar? Wasn't he coming? She hoped so. Talcor frightened her. He didn't seem to have any thread of kindness in him. At least Kytar had moments of kindness.

She'd just closed her eyes in a vain attempt to shut out the darkness and calm herself, when she heard the door open. Talcor entered the room. He stood shadowed in the doorway for a moment, just watching her. Her heart raced and even in the dim light, she was unable to hide her fear. He smiled at her then stepped aside and flicked on the lights.

Kytar entered the room and Marissa sighed in relief. She believed he'd protect her from Talcor until she saw the blackness of his eyes. *No*, she screamed silently, frightened by his implacable face. He walked toward her and not one line of his face softened as her eyes pleaded with him.

He stood at the head of the table, looking down at her. "Are you ready to submit to me?" he asked.

Something in the way he stood or maybe the fact of Talcor's presence against the wall caused her to hesitate rather than simply screaming out a no. After Talcor's treatment, she accepted her father's claims that Kytar had been kind.

Before she could respond to his question, he said, "You'll learn not to hesitate." He looked up at Talcor and nodded.

Talcor turned to the cabinet on the wall. Marissa's heart nearly stopped as she realized Talcor picked up a crop. Carrying the crop, he walked over to Kytar and handed it to him.

Talcor stood motionless while Kytar said, "I claim you as mine. You are my companion. I own your body. I own your mind. I own your spirit. I claim you as mine. I train you now to show the world our commitment is real. The ritual will prove that you may not challenge our link."

Talcor walked over to the side of the table. He held up nipple clamps. Dangling them in front of her eyes, a cruel smile broke across his face as he grabbed a breast. Hard fingers massaged her bruised breasts and Marissa arched off the table. And she opened her mouth to scream when he pulled her nipple out and attached a clamp but Talcor quickly grabbed her chin. "If you scream I'll gag you. Be silent. Get used to subservience. Your companion owns your body and he wants you to accept whatever he demands. He asked me to teach you about pain...are you hurting yet?" He watched her eyes as he reached down and flicked her adorned nipple.

She couldn't stop her sudden flinch.

"Good."

The second clamp seemed to hurt even more. She arched off the table, unable to stifle a moan. Kytar placed a hand on her forehead, giving her a moment to regain her breath. Once her breathing evened, he looked up at Talcor and nodded. "Continue."

Talcor pulled the restraints off her arms and legs. He caught Marissa's hands as she moved to free her breasts. "No, you do not want to do that," he said in a calm, reasonable voice that terrified her. Still holding her wrists in a tight, unbreakable grip, he pulled her upright and close. Her breasts pressed against his hard chest and the bones in her wrist threatened to give way.

Gasping from the shock of his ruthless actions, she tried to cope but he gave her no chance to recover. Pulling a rope out of his pocket, he bound her wrists and hung her from a hook far above her.

Marissa pulled her arms, trying to lower them to ease the sharp, stinging pull in her nipples. This new position caused the clamps to bite deep. Her vision dimmed and she was afraid she'd faint. She threw a glance at Kytar, pleading for him to help. His harsh eyes met hers.

"You demanded this, little one. Remember that."

Talcor grabbed her hair, forcing her head down toward the floor. "Lower your eyes," he said in a chilling voice.

Marissa did, frightened by the fact Kytar refused to help her.

Talcor cupped her breasts in his large hands, massaging them for a moment before turning his back on her. He walked to the cupboard and pulled out a length of rope. Walking back toward her, his evil smile told her she wouldn't like his next move. But she was helpless before the strength and determination of these two men.

Talcor circled the rope under her breasts, tight around her ribs until she couldn't take a deep breath. Still smiling, he started humming as he circled the rope again and again, above and below her nipples until her breasts were bound, pointing straight out, topped by the clamp like a candle on a cake. She moaned, trying to make herself invisible as Talcor bent and licked each nipple. Leaving them wet and glistening, he nodded to Kytar.

"Are you ready to submit to my will?" Kytar's eyes glittered like obsidian, unreadable and opaque.

"Don't do this," she whispered.

"You'll learn not to fight my will." Turning to Talcor, he said, "Take her to the wall."

Talcor started back. Even his cruelty had limits. "Kytar —"

"Now!"

Talcor shrugged and ignoring Marissa's feeble struggles, he lowered her arms and pulled her over to a wall. Shoving her against the rough stone, her breasts on fire, he grabbed an arm and pulled it high. The other arm quickly received the same treatment. He grabbed an ankle and Marissa tried to kick him, but his large hand held her immobile while he pulled her leg out. He quickly had both legs spread and bound. Marissa, pressed tight against the cold stone, shivered at the harsh touch against her nipples. She tried to lean back but couldn't move.

Kytar moved close behind her. His body pressed her against the stone. "Are you ready to submit to my will?" he whispered in her ear, sending a shiver down her back.

Unable to speak, she shook her head and felt her curls catch in his fingers. He used his grip in her hair to pull her head back. "That's my collar you wear. You will learn to respect my authority and value our link."

Then he let go and stepped away. The slash of the crop caught her by surprise. She screamed, not from the sting of the lash, but from the unexpected finger stroke to her clit that followed the slash. She lost track of time as he slashed and stroked. The pain and pleasure tangled in her mind. She couldn't tell one from the other as her breasts scraped the wall.

Overloaded by the sensations he generated, she couldn't stop the words that spilled out. "Take me, please just take me, I can't stand any more!" Marissa screamed at Kytar. Her pussy ached and throbbed, clenching on an emptiness that tormented her. She needed him and she ached for him. She needed him to fill her. She needed to feel his huge cock ramming against her cervix, all the way in, pinning her to the wall.

Kytar moved close behind her. "You are not in a position to demand anything," he said as he reached around and pulled off the clamps. Marissa screamed as sensation returned and blended with the slashes on her back. Her vision dimmed as the binding around her chest prevented a deep breath. She needed air. No, she needed Kytar. She sagged in the restraints, unable to stand. "Please, fill me..."

"No," Kytar whispered in her ear. Backing off, he ignored her shuddering need and left the room.

Talcor chuckled as he moved behind her and began undoing her restraints. "He's very good, isn't he?"

Marissa froze as she realized Talcor had witnessed her humiliation. How could Kytar have done that to her? She tried to pull away, but he ignored her feeble struggles as he removed her bindings and tied her to the table again. Then he turned off the lights and left too.

Marissa, aching and needy, groaned her disappointment. Kytar wasn't going to satisfy her no matter how much she pleaded. How much longer could she maintain her sanity in the face of his ruthless domination?

* * * * *

Talcor left the training room to find Kytar leaning against a wall. His hands on his knees, head down, he looked like he was in pain. "It is within the rules to take release with a slave."

Kytar threw a heated glance at Talcor. "That won't be necessary. Marissa will give me release tomorrow."

Talcor frowned. "She's not ready for that. You push too fast."

"If I don't push, neither one of us will survive this. Don't think I didn't notice your arousal."

Talcor shrugged and grinned. "She is beautiful, but just a little too willful even for my tastes. She is not bending, the way a woman should. At some point, she must surrender to you or the training may break her."

"I will not let that happen," Kytar said through gritted teeth. Straightening, he continued, "I appreciate your help. If you hadn't been there…"

"You have my loyalty. We'll continue tomorrow?"

Kytar nodded and watched Talcor leave.

* * * * *

Marissa awoke in the dark, at first not knowing where she was. Then the memory of her agonizing night returned and she realized location didn't matter. Spread naked on the table she felt like a virgin offering with her hands and feet bound.

She was the captive of a Darinthian male. The dark seemed to press down on her, as if holding her with a heavy hand. She struggled to remain calm, knowing hysterics would not help. Indeed, Kytar might like hysterics, she thought, as a panicked giggle escaped. After all, he and Davo had both warned her.

She hadn't really believed though. She hadn't realized how much power she'd handed him when she challenged him. Should she withdraw it? No! She would survive. Somehow she'd survive.

Bright light suddenly flooded the room. Slowly glancing out from behind her eyelids, she saw Talcor and Kytar enter the room.

Chapter Ten

Marissa watched Kytar and Talcor, fearing what new trial they had in store for her but relieved that Talcor carried a food tray. The scent went straight to her empty stomach. Talcor set the tray down and stood smiling at her. She broke his glance and looked at Kytar.

Kytar's naked chest, lined with solid muscle and a light covering of black hair, made Marissa's mouth water—at the same time she cursed her libido. How could a man who hurt her, who treated her as a possession, arouse her? How did he make her feel so safe even as he looked so dangerous?

Noticing her look, he smiled. It was not a nice or genuine smile, but a smile that terrified her. It was the smile of a man who knows his own power and strength, a man determined to win. A smile accompanied by gleaming black eyes that held no humor. He moved closer. "You'll eat when we're done. First tell me who you are," he demanded in that husky gentle voice that warned her to obey.

Marissa swallowed. Why the strange question? He knew who she was.

"My name is Mar—"

He grabbed her chin. "You are my companion," he stated, his gentle words belying his sudden action.

Marissa's heart nearly stopped at the intensity of his words. His onyx eyes pierced to her soul. Fighting would only delay the inevitable but she couldn't stop herself. "I am your slave," she argued, her voice shaky with fear.

He smiled and reached out to one of her breasts. His hand hovered over it, not touching. She watched as her nipple hardened as if to reach out to him. His other hand moved lower, one low stroke and he said, "You're dripping wet. You like what I do. I didn't think you would enjoy my training but you obviously want a strong man. Why continue resisting?"

Marissa's eyes widened, stunned by the reaction he'd created so effortlessly. She did want him. She couldn't deny that reality. She closed her eyes to shut out his satisfied expression. Lulled by the warmth of his hands, she heard him say, "You are my companion. While in training, your body belongs to me. It is mine to do with as I wish. Do you understand?"

She wanted to scream no. No, she didn't understand any of this. Instead, a gasp escaped her as need and arousal flooded deep within as he continued his gentle ministrations. Marissa gulped. He knew where and how to touch her. He understood her body better than she, who'd owned it for twenty-five years. She shuddered under his hands as she realized he would and could demand her willing compliance at every stage. She had no tools to fight him. She was helpless before his knowledge and a tiny part of her reveled in his power.

He smiled at her, his keen eyes showing his awareness of her struggle. His hands trailed outside her pelvic girdle and he leisurely continued his massage down the outside of her legs. When he reached her feet, he gave each one a gentle massage. Then he started up the inside of her legs. She tried to cringe, embarrassed by her naked, helpless exposure but she couldn't move and she watched him climb her body.

He reached the juncture of her thighs and gently parted her labia. He inserted a finger, just the tip and wiggled it a little. Suddenly he stopped and looked up at her. Watching her, waiting for her response, he inserted the tip of a second finger.

Focused on the movement between her legs, Marissa couldn't speak. She forgot Talcor's watching eyes. A delicious thrill fought through her fear. Kytar spread his fingers just a little, and then he started a deep stroke, massaging her channel. He bent down, blew on her clitoris. Stunned—as if from a blow—her mind stopped. He licked her clitoris and followed the lick with a gentle bite. Waves of pleasure shot through Marissa but he didn't let her come. Once more, he bit down on her clitoris, sending a wash of pain threading through the pleasure. She screamed when he stopped touching her, "Take me!"

"Are you aroused, little one? Do you still believe being my companion is a bad thing?"

He didn't wait as Marissa struggled to form an answer that wouldn't come.

"You're hesitating again. That's not allowed. You still have much to learn." He quirked an eyebrow. "Do you want me?" he asked and this time he waited for her answer.

"Yesss," she hissed.

He chuckled. "Any way I say. Any time I want. You are mine." And he once again bent to the task of bending her to his will. "Beg, little one. Beg me to satisfy you again," he said.

"Please," Marissa started, not certain if she begged for him to stop or to continue. She fell silent as a third finger entered her narrow channel.

He watched her eyes as he spread his fingers. Marissa's breathing hitched, held motionless in his control. Open and helpless. "Do you surrender to me?" he asked softly.

"I let you collar me! What more do you want?"

"I want your full surrender and acceptance, without hesitation or argument and I will have it."

He rotated his hand, just a little, back and forth. She clamped down on it, but he was stronger and she couldn't stop the motion, only feel him just at her entrance. She ached to feel him deeper.

He smiled as he withdrew his fingers one by one.

Marissa bit her lip to stop her scream of frustration.

His hand trailed along her cleft before he gently parted her lower lips once more. He used a finger to circle her clitoris, never quite touching, never quite giving her the pressure she needed to come again. Instead, as if winding a spring, he coiled the tension more. How taut could he make it before she broke? Repeatedly, he came near to satisfying her need before withdrawing. Marissa writhed on the table.

"Please…please just take me," she begged, unable to resist as mindless need and shudders of anticipation racked her body.

Kytar chuckled at her need and continued his work. Again and again, he brought her close, then retreated. As if from a great distance, Marissa heard him ask, "Do you begin to see, little one, why the women on Darinth do not struggle against their fate? And why your challenge will fail."

"Damn you," Marissa sobbed with need. And every time she believed she could stand no more, he proved her wrong. Her entire body clenched into one long strand of tension and she screamed at him, demanding satisfaction.

"Not yet, little one, don't be so anxious," he said. He climbed on the table and laid his weight on top of her.

His chest pressed down, forcing her into the hardness of the table. He framed her head with his hands. "Stop struggling," he commanded. "I know what you need and you'll receive it when I say."

The hardness of his body fueled need and panic, warring with her anger. How could he arouse her so easily? She fought to regain some measure of control. All the while, Kytar's black eyes watched.

Her breathing evened as she came off the peak.

Kytar murmured, "Good, little one, very good."

Then gave her a gentle kiss and climbed off her, leaving her shuddering.

Talcor freed her from the table. "You have five minutes to take care of your needs." Marissa stumbled to the bathroom before returning to eat the now cold food. She'd just finished when Talcor forced her to the table. He bound her extremities, turned out the lights and left her in the darkness, confused and still aroused. Angry, with herself as well as Kytar, she cursed her lust. Her stomach was full; she shouldn't feel so empty.

* * * * *

Kytar tossed back a drink. "I don't think I can survive her training."

"The binding...the binding really did overwhelm you?" Talcor asked hesitantly. Every male knew the binding was magic, but Talcor had always been able to resist taking the final step that had trapped Kytar.

"Oh, yes. I've had no choice since I first saw her."

Talcor grunted. "Doesn't sound pleasant."

"It will be. Once we finish the challenge ritual."

"You don't plan on taking the full two weeks, do you?"

"Even with your help, I can't survive two weeks. I ache to take her."

"But the risk..."

Kytar shrugged.

"You love this woman or you would not suffer so."

Kytar didn't reply.

"I'll do my best to guard you both," Talcor said softly.

Kytar nodded. "We'll give her an hour and then continue."

* * * * *

An hour later, they walked back into the playroom.

Marissa's closed eyes gave Kytar a twinge of anxiety. Was he pushing her too fast? He wished she didn't fight so hard. He wasn't going to let her win, but he hadn't expected her to be quite such a challenge.

121

He exchanged a glance with Talcor.

Talcor shrugged as if to say it was Kytar's choice.

Kytar closed his eyes for a moment, seeking a calm center. It wouldn't do to train Marissa while he still had doubts. He ruthlessly shoved aside his concern. He had to take the next step.

Kytar walked to the table.

Marissa's eyes popped open. She watched him walk around the table, releasing her restraints. He could almost feel her sigh of relief. She wouldn't feel so relieved if she knew what came next. Wrapping her hair in his hand, he forced her off the table and onto her knees.

"Look at me," he commanded. He saw her eyes stumbling a moment on his large bulge in front of her face before continuing up to his face. He held her eyes for a long minute.

"Suck me," he ordered, tightening his grip on her hair.

Marissa fantasized about sucking his cock, but not like this. She shuddered as his black eyes chilled her. She wanted to refuse his demand. But the tense line of his body told her she had no choice. She didn't like his attitude, but she couldn't deny that she wanted to taste him.

His cold gaze scored her as her trembling hands struggled with his pants fastener. He didn't help her. He just waited.

She gasped when she saw his size. Not only was his penis thick, it was long as well.

He tightened the hand holding her hair. "Suck me," he said in a husky tone that brooked no argument.

She swallowed hard and leaned forward. She licked the tip of his penis, tasting his salty, silky heat. She reached a hand to hold his burning shaft and felt the steel beneath. She opened her mouth and enclosed just the tip.

His hand tightened more. "Swallow all of it," he ordered.

She closed her eyes and tried. Her jaw stretched. The tip of his cock hit the back of her throat before she'd taken more than half his size. She raised her eyes, helplessly pleading.

He smiled. Holding her head, he nudged forward.

She couldn't breathe with him so deep. He pressed against the walls of her throat, widening her. She flushed in the face of his strength. Surprised by an intense contraction in her pussy she moaned. As he throbbed deep inside her throat, it seemed as though an electric current shot straight from her upper opening to her lower one.

She struggled to back off a little but he kept her head motionless. Dizziness assaulted her as her air ran out. Blackness encroached before he finally pulled back a little and she could breathe again. He let her draw a quick breath before forcing his way into her again.

"You'll learn to take all of me, easily and smoothly," he said as he repeated the pattern of burying himself deeply, holding and then letting her gasp a breath.

Marissa responded to his strength. The fire in her belly grew as he continued savaging her mouth. Every time he forced himself deep into her throat, an answering twinge jerked her empty cunt. Her nipples expanded, seeking a touch.

He ignored her needs, controlling her head, using her as a receptacle, until finally she felt a pulsing deep in her throat. She swallowed when he came, unable to do anything else since he shot himself so deep within her. Heat seared down her throat, causing her cunt to clench and throb. And when he yelled, "Come!", a roaring wave exploded through her body and she lost herself in its intensity.

He freed his hand from her hair and stepped back. In her exhaustion, she fell to the floor. Shuddering, she struggled to breathe past the ache he'd left and the intensity of her orgasm. He hadn't even touched her nipples or clit, how had she come so violently? Every muscle in her body felt the ache.

"Not bad, little one, but I know you can do better. We'll try again tomorrow."

His feet moved from her vision, replaced by Talcor's legs. Boneless and shaken, she didn't even think of fighting as Talcor picked her up.

* * * * *

She woke to find herself back in the bedroom. Davo stood by the side of the bed, just looking down at her.

"Father, help me..."

"Help you what?"

"Get me out of here. I can't take much more."

"It is far too late for me to help you. You should have called off the challenge when Kytar offered you the chance. Your only hope now is to submit to his will, to stop fighting him. If you don't, I fear he may break you. Accept Kytar as your companion."

Marissa wanted to scream at him. She couldn't stop. She couldn't just give up her freedom without a fight. "I..." Marissa trailed off, not knowing what to say. Her mind swam with conflicting desires that threatened to drown her.

Her father reached out and placed a hand on her shoulder. "Why do you keep fighting, child? If you're honest with yourself, you know you've never experienced such satisfying sex—sex that goes far beyond the simple physical scratching of your world. Forget your culture and feel what Kytar is doing. Can you deny that you feel the link and you want Kytar every bit as much as he wants you?"

"But...he frightens me," she said, barely whispering, afraid of admitting her weakness.

"But he also arouses you, doesn't he?"

Marissa closed her eyes and nodded, not able to voice the fact her father was right.

124

"You're not a failure because you respond to him. There is nothing wrong with responding to his strength. It's our way. Kytar only wants what is best for you. Trust him."

Marissa remained silent. She didn't know what to say to her father or how to cope with Kytar's challenge to her beliefs. Her world — the stable one she'd always known — vanished in a welter of needs that had nothing to do with rational thinking.

She heard her father leave the room. She wanted to call him back, but he couldn't or wouldn't help her. She had to face her demons alone. Why couldn't she just accept Kytar? He obviously wanted her. He wasn't happy about training her. He didn't enjoy hurting her, not the way her stepfather had enjoyed hurting her mother. Marissa knew beyond a doubt that Kytar was nothing like her stepfather. Tormented by the confusing knot of her thoughts, she curled up into a ball and tried to fall asleep.

* * * * *

Davo entered Kytar's study and poured himself a drink. Talcor sat in one chair while Kytar sat behind his desk.

Davo tossed back the drink. Looking at Kytar, he said, "She seems so fragile."

Kytar's mouth flattened. "You knew training would be hard. Her customs are so different from ours. But she is much stronger than she looks."

Davo raised his eyebrows. He waved toward Talcor. "You needed a watcher?"

"You know that is an acceptable custom."

"I'm just a little surprised."

"So was I. Marissa's defiance undoes me."

Davo started a little. His eyes widened at Kytar's admission.

Kytar gave a bitter laugh. "Yes, the training affects both of us. I'd heard tales, but not realized just how hard it would be to keep her chaste."

"How far along are you?"

Talcor answered, "They've survived the lash and oral sex. She comes on command."

Dave shook his head, frowning. He said, "You've still to breach her rectum? Or command her compliance?"

"I'm well aware of the tasks left," Kytar replied in a tight voice.

"You could stop anytime. Just release her," Davo said.

"Never." Kytar's eyes glittered. "That will never happen. Marissa's challenge will fail."

"I don't like seeing her like this."

"And you think I do? I've pledged to protect her. I've never treated a companion so harshly. I want to soothe her fears. I want to satisfy her needs. I ache constantly and long to consummate our binding."

"What if she rescinds her challenge?"

"Did she?"

"No," Davo sighed. "I tried, but she's determined."

"Good, because at this point, so am I. You were right, Davo. She must accept our link no matter how hard it is on both of us. Her training progresses and she's beginning to understand how much her beliefs limit her responses. She can go further. She can go all the way and so can I. She will submit to me."

* * * * *

"Do you trust me?"

Kytar's voice roused Marissa from her slumber. She stared up at his chocolate eyes. Trust, what was trust? She trusted him to feed her and let her eventually use a bathroom.

126

She trusted him to arouse her as no man had before. She trusted him not to permanently damage her. She trusted him to be in control simply because he took all of hers.

She had to trust him since he dominated her so easily. Did she trust him to treat her like an equal? No. Never. But then she wasn't his equal, was she? She'd never be equal while he could test and challenge her and never break a sweat. She did trust him not to break her. She did trust him to give her violently satisfying orgasms. She felt a hairline fracture run through a mental barrier she hadn't known existed. Startled by its presence, she realized she'd built it against her stepfather and used it against all men. But Kytar was not her stepfather.

"Answer me, little one. Do you trust me?" he demanded, bringing her out of her head.

"Yes," she sighed past the lump in her throat.

He gave a half-smile and sat on the edge of the bed. Reaching out, he stroked her cheek and before she could stop herself, she turned into his hand.

"Today will challenge you as never before," he said.

Her eyes widened. "I don't think I can take much more..."

"You'll take all I give, little one," he whispered, climbing in bed with her.

The kiss was soft, a gentle brush of their lips. But it quickly intensified as he thrust into her mouth. Plundering deep inside, she melted even as her mind screamed to resist, but she told it to shut up. She didn't want to fight Kytar anymore and the hairline fracture widened. She admitted that she wanted to take everything he demanded. She wanted to give him everything he needed. And she didn't want him to stop.

He took her air and her will once again. He kissed her into soft compliance. His body, hard and lean, felt like a furnace warming her.

"Kytar!" Talcor's voice cut through the kiss like a knife.

As if drugged, Kytar slowly broke the kiss. Resting his forehead against Marissa's, he shuddered. His arousal pressed against her belly. Why did Talcor stop him? She felt his need, as great as hers was. Why didn't he take her? Why did he leave her unfulfilled? "Just take me," she whispered.

Raising his head, she saw his eyes black and glittering with need.

"Just take me," Marissa repeated, staring into his dark eyes.

"Kytar?"

Kytar turned his head to glare at Talcor. He drew in a deep breath and nodded. Then he moved off Marissa, leaving her exposed to the cold air.

"No," she screamed, "don't leave me like this."

"I'm not leaving." A bitter laugh escaped as he moved back. "We're not done yet."

Marissa sprang from the bed, grabbing him. "Please," she begged, winding her arms around his neck. He easily caught her wrists and held her still. He gave her a quick hug before throwing her back on the bed. "Stay there," he commanded.

"No! I'm sorry! I call off my challenge! I can't take any more. Kytar I need you."

Chapter Eleven

ᴙᴏ

Marissa's words froze Kytar.

"Kytar, please," she begged, her mouth swollen from his kisses, her hair disheveled. Stunningly beautiful, he wanted nothing more than to accept her surrender.

"I witness her withdrawal," Talcor said from the doorway, his voice tense but Kytar knew Talcor wouldn't interfere. He'd accept Kytar's decision no matter which way it went.

Kytar could end this now and consummate their union. The thought tempted him. But then he remembered her resistance and her defiance.

Was her withdrawal of the challenge simply one more tactic to control their relationship? If he surrendered now, he knew her defiance would come back. She'd resort to claims of trickery and she'd continue to fight. She may have withdrawn her challenge, but she still hadn't acknowledged his power over her or their link. And she still hadn't said she loved him.

"Do you submit to me?" he asked in a voice harsh with frustration and anger.

She hesitated.

"That's what I thought. I refuse to stop the challenge, little one. We will finish the charade you started. One way or the other we will complete the challenge. I won't accept a bond with a companion who believes she doesn't want to be with me." He turned and walked to the small table holding various objects.

She started to move off the bed toward Kytar but Talcor moved forward. His hard eyes, glittering with anger and satisfaction, kept her pinned to the bed as he said, "Let the challenge continue."

Marissa bit her lip. How could Kytar throw her offer back in her face? Was that what he felt when she challenged him? The thought startled her. Did he feel rejected? Marissa turned her head to watch him.

No other lover had aroused her to the point of mindless passion the way he did. If she was honest with herself, she had to admit she wanted to feel his power. She'd never dreamed how safe and protected a powerful man would make her feel. She wanted to rebel against that thought, to reject it, but she couldn't. Kytar was nothing like her stepfather. He wasn't cruel. She saw his agony and concern while he trained her. He loved her. Did she also love him?

She couldn't answer that question, but the wall deep inside was now riddled with cracks. Withdrawing her challenge had changed her. All of a sudden, her continued resistance seemed foolish. Why was she trying to free herself when all she really wanted was Kytar? She could feel their link and it no longer frightened her. Instead, she reveled in the link, knowing she would never be alone again. Why had she started this foolish challenge? Why had she made it so hard on both of them? Little wonder Kytar didn't trust her change of heart. She'd given him no reason to believe she would ever accept him.

Kytar took a few deep breaths, calming his racing heart before turning back to her. "Today we work on obedience. Submission increases your arousal. I'm going to teach you things about your body. Things you never knew. Things you don't think possible. I'm leaving you unbound," he continued. "You will stay still for me," he stated in a tone that brooked no disobedience. "Turn over."

"But I withdrew my challenge. I'll do what you say."

"Then do it. Without comment. You will stay silent, no matter what I do."

She looked up at him, confused and angered by his cold tone.

"Turn over, little one, on your stomach."

She slowly rolled over. Her hands clenched in fists beneath her breasts, her legs closed tight, her buttocks clenched. His hand traced her ass. Then he lightly spanked her.

"Spread your legs wide," he said.

She hesitated rather than complying.

Talcor didn't tolerate her resistance. He grabbed an ankle and moved one leg from the comfort of the other. Then he took her second leg and moved it as well. "Obey your companion or I will help you obey."

Talcor's threatening words chilled Marissa, freezing her protest.

"Much better," Kytar murmured. He gave her a stinging slap, followed rapidly by three more. She gasped as warmth flowered across her buttocks.

"Just a few more," Kytar said, following his words with action.

Marissa tucked her head into the bed, trying to figure out her conflicting emotions. Her heated behind didn't really hurt, she was more shocked than hurt. She heard Kytar move off for a moment. She didn't hear him come back, but she felt a stinging slash across her labia. She winced at the unexpected pain and then moaned when a finger trailed down to her clit. Warmth flooded her pussy and she clenched her muscles, trying to stop the moisture leaking out.

"Put your arms above your head," Kytar commanded.

Wanting to obey him, to prove her change of heart, she slowly raised her arms, but her hands were stiff-fisted.

A second lash fell, then a third and fourth. Kytar's hands once more traced the marks he left. "Open your hands. Unclench your fists," he ordered.

"I can't..." she tried to protest, but the sting of the lash fell on her ass.

"Unclench your fists," he ordered again. "Lie open and unresisting."

She gritted her teeth and did as he commanded. Shudders racked her body. The pain stung like sharp arrows and she feared what he'd do next, she was so vulnerable in this position. He surprised her by lightly tracing her clit and the pain was lost in pleasure. She forgot the pain. She was close to coming when he stopped.

"Stay still," he commanded as he moved off for a moment.

Groaning into the pillow, she started to look up but he repeated, "Stay still."

His hands massaged her ass as if to rub her pain even deeper. Once again, a hand slipped to her clit. A finger in her channel aroused her even while his other hand continued massaging. His hair fell on her ass as he bent his head and licked the lash marks. The gentle strokes of his tongue and hand contrasted with the burning throb of the marks. Even when he used his teeth and gently bit her ass, she couldn't stop the wetness that seeped down her cunt. She moaned, needing more than this gentle torture.

She started when a finger slid into her rectum. "No..." she whispered.

"No man has ever played with this channel?"

"Please..."

"Little one, you don't know what you've been missing. Don't move," he commanded as he massaged her opening with a cold jelly.

She squirmed when the pressure started.

Kytar smacked her ass with the flat of his hand. "Hold still."

She tried, but as the cold relentless pressure built, sending shards of indescribable pleasure and pain, she clenched her buttocks.

"No," Kytar commanded, smacking her ass again. "Hold still. Do not move. Stay open for me."

"I can't," Marissa moaned. "It's too much."

"You can and you will submit to me," Kytar said.

Marissa shuddered at the hardness in his voice. He held the pressure steady, waiting for her response. The light touch in her mind was barely noticeable as she fought her instincts. Breathing deeply of his cedar scent, she calmed and stilled beneath his waiting hand.

The pressure increased.

Her breath hitched as she expanded. "No…" she moaned.

"Relax," he said, "take deep breaths. Open for me and it will hurt less."

A sharp pain signaled his implacable decision to breach her virgin rectum. She was close to screaming when the pressure lessened as he pulled the implement out a little.

"Breath deeply, little one. This is very small. When I take you, then you can scream."

His implied threat startled her. She'd never be able to take his width.

"Don't tense."

She tried to take deep breaths, to still her tightness and relax against his assault. The pressure started again and she widened. Ignoring her groans, he kept up his relentless force as the object moved deeper and deeper, millimeter by millimeter.

Her eyes rolled as she struggled to cope with the intensity of the sensations washing through her body. It felt good. It felt strange. She needed to scream. She needed the pressure released. But he kept up the relentless demand that her channel widen more until the thing was firmly seated, deep within.

All her attention focused on the new sensation. She wasn't aware of Talcor moving to each corner of the bed and binding her extremities. He covered her with a blanket, while Kytar laid a hand on her shoulder and said, "Rest awhile, little one, and adjust to your position. We're nearly done."

She closed her eyes, feeling the object deep within and her only regret was that her cunt was empty. The pulse in her bottom and the sharp stripes on her back, blended into an aching need that tightened her empty cunt into one aching mass of need. She floated on the sensations, following one then the other, letting them wash through her taking her away from all conflict. No tormented protest filled her mind, no endless loop of her mother's degradation played in her head. For once, Marissa was at peace.

She returned to the awareness of the anal plug sliding out. Warm hands massaged her back, rubbing a numbing lotion into her bruises. She sighed with pleasure, curling to his touch, grateful for the release from stimulation, if only for a few moments. He kissed along her shoulder, then leaned down to finish unbinding her.

"Turn over," he murmured in her ear before raising up enough to let her move.

Marissa rolled over slowly, startled when she noticed Talcor silently standing guard at the door. Why was he always there? She didn't voice the question though. She did as Kytar asked.

She lay on her back, looking up into Kytar's eyes. Mindless, she didn't even wonder what he might do next. He gazed deeply into her soul and gauged her for the next step. He moved next to her. Propping his head on one hand, he reached the other toward her breast. He waved his hand above her and her nipple reached out as if to feel his touch. As her need expanded, he kept his hand just out of reach. Then he did the same with the other nipple until both reached for the ceiling.

"You want me," he stated. "You like what I do, little one."

Unable to argue with the evidence her body provided and tired of fighting her responses, she shrugged.

Removing his hand from above her nipples, he laid his arm alongside his body and looked at her. She remained motionless and quiet, simply waiting for his next move. She startled herself by hoping he'd take her now to that place he'd shown her, the one where she was mindless with need and longing.

"Who are you?" he asked.

"Your companion," Marissa replied without hesitation or pause. Then realizing what she'd said her eyes widened. Should she deny it? He'd proven the fact and she was startled to realize she no longer wanted to deny the truth, her body couldn't lie. She wanted this man in every way possible. Any way he said. She needed his strength, strength that could send her winging out of control. She'd never experienced anything like the sensations he created.

"Do you submit to me?"

"Yes," she replied without hesitation.

"Talcor wants you. Should I let him satisfy his lust for you?" Kytar asked softly.

"What?" she stammered, not quite comprehending the question.

"Talcor, do you want him?" he demanded again.

Marissa struggled to make sense of his question. "But I'm your companion," she automatically replied. "I don't want another man."

He laughed and stroked her face. "Excellent. I'm proud of the progress you're making," he said. Leaning forward, he captured her lips. His hands moved firmly on her breasts, wrenching a moan of need from her throat.

"Will you obey me during the ritual?" he asked, whispering into her ear.

"Yes," she moaned. A thrill of fear paralyzed her when the words sunk in. Could she obey him as mindlessly as the ritual apparently demanded? She longed to have him take her fear but before she could voice her concern, she heard Talcor say, "I witness the surrender."

Stunned, she looked at Kytar. Why were Talcor's words so formal? What now? Before she could panic though, Kytar stood and swept her into his arms. Carrying her into the bathroom, he sat her on the edge of the tub and ran water for a bath.

Despite the cold of the tub, Marissa sat quiet and complacent. What was happening to her? She'd lost all her desire to fight. For the first time since she'd met him, she reached out to him, touching his shoulder.

He stiffened under her hand, slanting a questioning glance back at her.

"I...I'll do my best for you..." She stumbled over the words.

Kytar smiled, engulfing her in a feeling of safety. "I know you will. Now relax," he said, as he helped her into the tub. "I'll be back in a little while."

Marissa slowly sank into the hot water, reveling in its heat. She couldn't figure out what had happened. She attempted to dismiss Darinthian practices as abhorrent and degrading but instead she felt safe and satisfied though they hadn't yet consummated their bond. Maybe this world *was* magic. She felt no desire to fight. The depressing weight in her head was gone, her mental barriers shattered by her need for Kytar. She felt like she could fly, she was so free.

Kytar hadn't broken her spirit. Instead, he'd demolished her fears and anger. And she realized her need to be free at any cost carried a high penalty. She'd found true freedom and safety with Kytar, a freedom she never imagined or known existed.

She was so busy fighting that she'd ignored all her own needs and desires. Kytar hadn't broken her, he'd set her free. The fact that Kytar claimed control meant that she could lose all restraint. She didn't have to decide what to do next. Kytar would take care of that and she had to admit that for the first time in her life she felt free just to be herself. She didn't have to fight. She didn't have to think and that was a heady feeling especially when she felt cherished as well. Then her head cleared a little. She remembered her mother's letter. Her letter had talked about the freedom she'd find here. Is this what she meant? If so, how had she ever left?

Marissa felt a twinge of regret for her mother's loss. For the first time in Marissa's life, she belonged, really belonged. Cherished and not alone, she'd never be alone again. She'd always be with Kytar. That thought originally so horrifying now made her happier than she'd thought possible. The stunning realization that she loved Kytar caught her off guard and she wasn't prepared for his return.

"Little one," Kytar said, returning to sit on the edge of the tub, "look at me."

Marissa slowly opened her eyes and turned her head to look up at him, not quite ready to admit her love.

"I've called for the ritual tomorrow."

His words chilled her. The ritual was so unnecessary now. "I've surrendered. Do we really need to do this?"

"You know we do. Right now, you're compliant and willing. We both know that won't last long." He smiled down at her. "The ritual will strengthen our link to the point where even you will no longer be able to deny it."

"But I'm not denying it anymore. Isn't that what you wanted?"

"That's only part of what I want," he said, terminating further discussion by reaching out a hand, "time to get out."

Marissa let him take her hand and help her out of the tub. Still shaky and weak, mentally and physically, she wasn't sure she could have managed on her own. And when he pulled her close, his male scent enveloped her and despite her misgivings, she sank into the safety of his arms. His cedar scent comforted her, his strength fueled hers.

Kytar wrapped a towel around her cooling body. He dried her then helped her to the bedroom and said, "I won't see you again until the ceremony. Rest now. You'll need your strength tomorrow."

Marissa lay on the bed, eyes wide and unseeing. Her thoughts circling endlessly, trying to figure out what had changed. She wanted Kytar to take her in every way possible. She tried to lie to herself, by saying that he'd simply brainwashed her, but she accepted that wasn't true. She liked his strength, no matter how much she tried to deny it. The connection between them was undeniable. How could it strengthen? She should be horrified, rather than aroused, but she didn't care.

On her home world, she'd taken great pride in always being in control. Now, she found to her surprise that she enjoyed submitting to Kytar. She wanted him in any way he demanded. She was like those women in the vids. Cherished, as well as tormented. He tangled her emotions, creating combinations of sensations that caused her to explode in mindless frenzies. No other man had aroused her like this. Even the memories left her weak and needy.

What was going to happen tomorrow? Her father said the ritual was public. The thought of surrendering in public terrified her. Would she break? Would she fail Kytar? How could she have been so stupid as to demand any Darinthian ritual? she berated herself. It would have been so much easier just to accept Kytar without all this turmoil. Finding no comfort in her pointless wishes, she finally fell into a fitful sleep.

Talcor and a strange man were in the bedroom when she awoke. Marissa started. She wanted Kytar, she wanted to tell him she loved him but before she could speak, Talcor held up a hand. "It is time for the ritual."

Chapter Twelve

❧

The two men stared at her, their faces serious and intent.

"Get up," the stranger said.

Frightened by their harsh expressions and his cold tone, she sat up and swung her legs over the side of the bed.

Leather thongs hung from their belts and not one trace of sympathy or kindness crossed their faces.

"Kneel!" Talcor commanded.

Knowing that Talcor wouldn't hesitate to use force and uncertain as to whether or not this was part of the challenge ritual, Marissa said, "I'll obey." She moved without hesitation into the position he indicated.

"Yes, you will," Talcor replied. He moved close to her, his crotch just millimeters from her face. He cupped her chin and raised her head. He touched the collar encircling her throat, making sure it was snug. She would not be able to forget she wore it. Then he stepped back and the other man moved behind her.

He seized both of her wrists and twisted them harshly behind her. The leather cut into her wrists and she bit back a moan. Then they blindfolded her and forced a gag into her mouth.

Fear threatened to overwhelm Marissa. She couldn't give in to it. Bound helplessly before them, fear would send her into a blind panic from which there would be no escape. Even chained in the cell she hadn't felt as helpless as she did now. These men were frightening.

In a harsh voice, Talcor ordered, "Stand!" But she was too stunned and disoriented to do it on her own and his hand was gentle as he helped her to her feet. The stranger moved to her other side and they led her out of the room.

They walked for a long time. At least the time seemed long with her eyes covered, arms bound and mouth gagged. It was as if time altered and each moment expanded by hours. She didn't know how long they actually walked.

The men's tight grip on her arms helped her keep her feet when she stumbled. She was grateful for their strength even though she should be angry or defiant. But she was too confused to fight. Besides, fighting wouldn't help her. All she could hope for at this point was to maintain her dignity and submit to the coming ordeal with pride and grace. She finally admitted that it was her own fault she was in this position. Kytar and Davo had both given her the opportunity to escape the coming ordeal. All she could do now was endure it.

They entered a large space echoing with tension.

Talcor placed a hand on each shoulder and pushed her down. "Kneel," he commanded in a loud voice. Then he bent to her ear and whispered, "Trust Kytar."

She startled at the kindness in his voice. Kindness wasn't a quality she associated with Talcor. But before she could process his strange act, a hand pressed her legs apart. "Spread your legs," the other man commanded.

She lost her balance as she struggled to comply. Talcor steadied her by holding her shoulders, while the other man positioned her legs. She ended up with her knees nearly two feet apart.

Immediately, her thigh muscles protested the position. Unsteady and unbalanced, she wondered how long she'd be able to hold this position as their hands fell away from her and she fought to remain upright.

"Let the ritual begin," she heard a booming voice say.

A hand between Marissa's shoulder blades pushed her head to the floor. An easier position on her muscles, but more frightening in that it left her bottom high in the air and spread wide open. She could feel her labia trying to close and hide her exposure, but shelter was impossible in this position.

Someone moved around her, circling her. A hand barely brushed her ass then she heard a whistle and felt the sting of a lash. Before she could jerk out of position a hand cupped her head, keeping it down, and she heard Kytar whisper, "Don't move!"

Irrationally, a sense of relief poured through her. No matter what she faced, Kytar was close. He'd keep her safe. Another lash, this one caught her labia and she couldn't prevent the moan that escaped around her gag, but she held her position. She wanted to fight, but a barrier in her mind seemed to distance her from Kytar's actions.

She held still as a finger traced the lash mark, unfairly generating warmth in her pelvis. The lashings continued, interspersed with soft touches that aroused her.

Pain and pleasure mingled until she could not tell them apart. She was open for him to see her glistening wetness. She lost track of the number of strokes she received. By the time he stopped she was shuddering and trembling, struggling to hold her position.

"The first stage is complete," she heard the booming voice announce.

She briefly wondered how many stages there were, but the question fled as Kytar touched her.

Kytar seized her shoulders and raised her torso back to the agonizing position of kneeling with her legs apart. Kytar removed the gag. "Don't move. Stay silent," he encouraged her again.

She blinked in the harsh light when he removed her blindfold. She drew in a horrified breath when she realized she was in an auditorium. Beyond the glare of the spotlights, she could make out the shadowy forms of tier after tier of people. Men, she assumed. She doubted that any other women were present.

The men stayed so silent she hadn't realized they had such a large audience. Marissa cringed as she realized they'd witnessed her arousal. Stiffening her spine, she shoved aside the thought. She had to concentrate to survive what ever came next.

Kytar moved in front of her, cutting off her view of the audience. He kept one hand on her shoulder and one on her head. His hands didn't comfort her though. Strong, forceful and tense, prepared to force her compliance if she panicked.

The hand on her head moved and he wound her hair in a familiar grip. "Suck me," he demanded in a voice that carried to the rafters.

Once more, he showed no mercy as he shoved his cock deep into her throat. She was grateful he hadn't attached nipple clamps. She had enough to cope with. Clamps would have challenged her limits.

He forced himself deep into her throat until the connection between her throat and pelvis ignited. Her cunt ached in time with his thrusts. She wanted him down below, but he continued working himself in and out of her mouth. Her eyes closed, she relaxed into his grip, allowing another millimeter of depth. She forgot her audience, lost in sensation.

Her throat and jaw ached by the time he finally shot his come deep into her throat. There was no question of swallowing his ejaculation, he was far too deep to do else but swallow with her battered and bruised throat. She was breathless and a little dizzy by the time he finished and just a little cheated that he hadn't told her to come.

He'd simply used her, as if she were a convenient receptacle for his need, with no concern for her desires. She could feel the moisture seeping down her thighs and a tiny piece of her mind raged at his treatment. She needed him, buried not in her throat but deep in her pussy.

"The second stage is complete," the booming voice rang out.

Kytar moved behind her and freed her wrists.

Marissa groaned with pain as needles of circulation returned to her hands.

Kytar placed a hand on her head as a man rolled out a table. The table had just a little arch, with extensions…for her extremities, she realized with a cringe of fear. Kytar did not let her fear take hold though. With a sudden motion, he picked her up and placed her facedown on the table, quickly spreading her extremities, and tying her motionless.

The padding pushed against her belly. She couldn't prevent a small squirm; the pressure was tantalizing, but in the wrong spot. He circled to her head. Holding her face, he once again whispered, "You're doing well."

She relaxed a little at his words, glad that she pleased him. But his next words sent a thrill of fear through her, "Just hang on, little one. Don't move. Be very quiet no matter what happens."

He raised the table to cock height, and then turned it, fully exposing Marissa's nether regions to the large audience. Her face flamed, embarrassed by her public viewing. She'd wanted him to shield her from public view, but he had other plans.

He stood by the side of the table. The warm hard tip of a finger pressed against her rectum. "No…" she whispered.

"Quiet," he whispered back, continuing the preparation.

The first finger didn't hurt too much. "Relax," he commanded in a voice so soft it wouldn't reach the watching men. She tried to do as he ordered, but the second finger hurt more and she groaned, surrendering to the erotic feelings he created.

She was unprepared for the intensity of the sensations washing through her. He could effortlessly create pain that morphed into pleasure. And once more, he seemed determined to prove to her that pain and pleasure were two sides of the same coin. He didn't stop. He didn't hesitate. The pain of expansion and the pleasure of penetration increased as he forced three fingers inside. Then he withdrew his fingers and spread more of the cold jelly. He reinserted his fingers. Spreading them, he opened her wide. Then he twisted them around, massaging her opening.

The fourth finger hurt more. A sharp pain announced that her anus had stretched to its limits. She tried to squirm, to escape his relentless attentions, but she couldn't move. He forced his fingers in and out, again and again. The pain lessened as he continued the massage but when he spread his fingers wide, she couldn't stop the groan that escaped her throat.

Before she could assimilate the pain, he took his fingers out. The relief was instantaneous, despite the throbbing ache he'd left behind. She was just adjusting to the relief of an empty rectum when the hard tip of his cock touched her anal ring.

She felt a light breeze in her mind, whispering to her, telling her to relax and open for him. Mindlessly, she obeyed and Kytar, in one smooth motion, sank deep within her, filling her bottom with his hot strength. All of her attention focused inward, on her filled bottom and empty cunt.

She'd forgotten the audience until the sonorous voice boomed out, "The third stage is complete."

Chapter Thirteen

ॐ

Kytar pulled out of her, replacing his warmth with a cold plug. He unbound her, flipped her over and rebound her so fast that she'd barely realized what he was doing.

The table arched against her back. She cringed when she realized he planned to leave the plug in her butt. The foreign object kept her channel open, but pain blended with need and the emptiness in her cunt intensified, nearly causing her to scream for satisfaction.

Spread out like a sacrificial offering, every man in the room could see the glittering wetness of her arousal. A strange small part of her felt proud that she'd survived to this point. She couldn't deny her arousal.

"The woman has never been penetrated by a Darinthian. She is deemed chaste," the booming voice announced.

Marissa heard pleased murmurs from the audience, followed by excited chattering. She did not understand why the announcement caused so much excitement. She didn't care. By this time, despite the exhaustion deep in her bones, all she could focus on was Kytar and her need for him.

Despite the degradations—or maybe because of them— she desperately needed release. Hysteria threatened to overwhelm her. Everyone she knew thought her controlling. If they could only see her now, desperate for a release, they'd know she wasn't in control at all.

She bit her lip. She had to hold out. She loved Kytar. If she broke, so did their bonds and the thought of being free of him was no longer attractive. It horrified her to think that if she failed him, she'd destroy them both. Taking a deep breath, she focused. She was strong. She could survive this and then they'd always be together.

Kytar turned the table a little and brought over a stand. Suddenly a screen flickered to life and she saw her open, gaping, glistening pussy on a twenty-foot screen above. Clearly visible to every man in the audience, it revealed the truth of her need.

She was on fire. Her vagina ached with emptiness and the fullness in her rectum merely accentuated the emptiness in other places. Even her mouth longed for Kytar's cock if it meant she could have him inside her.

She hoped the next stage would be the breaching, but Kytar dashed that desire.

The camera remained fixed on her pussy as Kytar moved to her breasts. He lightly grazed his hand over her nipples and defying gravity, they stood high and proud. She saw another drop of moisture seep down the screen and she moaned when she realized he planned to arouse her even more and that her arousal would be on display for all to see.

Kytar left her nipples and circled each breast with a hand. He squeezed and massaged them, causing the blood to seek his touch. Then he left them — aroused and proudly pointing to the ceiling, aching for more — while he reached in a pocket and drew out the familiar gold clamps. She grew even wetter, moisture trailing down her thighs.

Kytar bent his head and licked a nipple. Then biting lightly, he pulled on the nipple and to Marissa's amazement it stretched even higher. When he was satisfied it would go no further, he clamped it in place.

Marissa tried to jerk away from the sharp, stabbing pain in her chest. He finished clamping her other breast. She closed her eyes and softly moaned. Her body was a waiting receptacle, under his complete command.

Marissa struggled to open her eyes. Her cunt, well lubricated by her need, wanted — no, needed — to be fucked.

She wanted more. She wanted Kytar deep inside. How much longer could he deny her? Unable to move away from the butt plug or the clamps, she wanted more. She silently cursed her need. She wanted her emptiness filled. She lay there quietly and silently, waiting for Kytar's next move.

He surprised her by saying, "Do you submit to my will?"

"Yes, I submit to your will," she replied without hesitation, floating on the bed of sensation he'd created. She shoved aside the tiny voice in her head that screamed a refusal. She didn't want to listen to that voice anymore. Kytar might hurt her, but he never abused her. He wasn't like her stepfather.

"Do you open yourself to me?"

"I am open to you." Again, she replied without hesitation, almost as if the words had grown in her mind, just waiting for an opportunity to speak them.

"Do you give me your will and your mind?"

"My will and my mind are yours. I love you."

Kytar stilled, staring down at her, stunned by her admission—a very public admission. A wave of lust and love poured through him. He started to reach for her bindings.

"The fourth stage is complete," boomed the voice.

The voice recalled him to his task. He shook his head. He'd nearly broken. But he couldn't, not yet. The ceremony wasn't finished. He had to finish.

Clenching his jaw, he moved to the head of the table. Framing her face in his hands, he bent over and his eyes held hers.

At first, it was like a rustling wind in her head. Then he blasted past all her barriers. She screamed with shock as he forcefully entered her mind, shoving aside her mental walls as if they were paper.

Nothing in her past had prepared her for the mental strength of the Darinthian male in the throes of ritual. He was deep inside her mind. He caressed some thoughts and shoved others aside as he sought out the strands he needed. He held her in thrall, finding the center of her pain and pleasure.

Her arousal built as he played in her mind. He built it higher and higher, never granting her release. He wound her like a coiled spring until she dreamed of exploding. She wanted to explode. She forgot the audience in her storm of need. Held helpless in his thrall, she didn't notice the first man approach. And she nearly screamed when he licked her clitoris.

She tried to push past the peak, but Kytar stopped her, ruthlessly quashing her arousal. "Not yet, little one," he murmured, a frown of concentration lining his face.

The second man approached Marissa and grazed a finger across her clitoris. Again, Kytar quashed her arousal. The third man licked a nipple. Still Kytar held her firmly in his grip. She began to realize why women could lose their minds during testing.

One after another, the strangers touched her. She was so close to the brink that without Kytar's strength, any one of those touches could have sent her over the edge, but he didn't let that happen, instead the relentless touches continued.

One man inserted two fingers in Marissa's vaginal canal and spread her outer lips. One man rotated the butt plug. Another man blew across her clitoris, yet another jiggled her nipple clamps. Some men stroked or licked her abdomen.

All the while, Kytar's gaze held her eyes and his mind controlled her, firmly commanding her body's response with mental touches. She was cherished and loved, he reminded her as he touched her mind, sometimes lightly, sometimes with more power, always there, never leaving her alone.

On and on it went, as all the hundreds of men in the auditorium came onstage to touch her. No part of her body escaped their attentions. Her ears were licked, nibbled and blown into. Her neck was bitten, her bellybutton filled by a finger and a firm hand below massaged her abdomen, leaving an aching in her belly that remained throughout the rest of the torture, every breath reminding her she could not fight these men. Would the ritual never end?

The line of men ceased. Still Kytar's eyes held her on the peak of release for an endless moment before she felt the soft stroke in her head as he said, "Come."

Marissa's world exploded. Her mind blasted apart in the intensity of her orgasm. Even Kytar's help couldn't prevent her scream as long, powerful contractions pulled on every muscle of her body and a throbbing release overwhelmed her.

She came back to awareness, still bound to the table. Her rectum had torn a little in the violence of her release. Still clamped, her nipples were painfully sensitive and she could still feel the touch of all those men.

"The fifth stage is complete," she heard and groaned. She didn't think she could withstand much more. Despite her orgasm, her cunt screamed for Kytar to fill her, she'd never be complete without him. *Would he never penetrate her?* Weakness seeped deep into the core of both her mind and her body. Her sanity wavered in and out, never quite solidifying.

Marissa clung to Kytar. His gaze holding her firmly, he was her reality. She feared what would happen when he left her mind.

But he didn't leave. Kytar held her as others removed the clamps from her breasts and then the plug. Finally, they freed her hands and ankles. She lay still, afraid to move. She feared there would be more and she feared there would be no more. Wasn't he ever going to fuck her?

Kytar took away the hysteria, filling her with a calm acceptance. Even with his help, she didn't think she could take much more.

Almost done, he whispered in her mind.

Her eyes widened and she saw a gleam of satisfaction race through his eyes. She heard him in her mind, *Say the following, out loud.* "I am Kytar's companion and we are bound forever — physically, mentally and spiritually."

"I..." She started to say but her voice broke. Swallowing past the lump in her still sore throat, she tried again, "I am Kytar's companion and we are bound forever — physically, mentally and spiritually." She spoke softly, but her voice echoed in the auditorium. Everyone heard.

"The sixth stage is complete," boomed the voice she was growing to hate.

Kytar's voice rang out as he said, "The challenge ritual is complete. We are bonded companions. We are one body, one mind, one spirit."

A scream ripped from her sore throat as deep within a band of pressure exploded. But the pressure didn't hang on the peak this time. Satisfaction flooded every piece of Marissa's body.

"The challenge to your link has failed. The bonds between Kytar and Marissa are recognized!" the voice announced, finally sounding excited. The entire auditorium broke into cheering at the announcement.

A wash of pride mingled with frustration. *Don't these men ever just fuck?* Despite her orgasms, she still craved Kytar's cock buried as deeply as it could go.

Kytar's chuckle filled her mind as he answered silently, *Your physical breaching is a private act. Don't worry. We will get to that point soon.* He smiled down at her and gently kissed her forehead, then turned to accept the acclaim of his fellow Darinthians.

He kept a hand on her shoulder and she closed her eyes. Feeling battered and bewildered, she gladly accepted his touch, too confused to try to sit or stand. She didn't want to see the men who had done intimate things to her. And she wanted to enjoy the feeling of joy that suffused her.

She would never have to say no again. She'd never be alone again. Peace flooded and calmed her exhausted body.

Confident that Kytar would keep her safe, she fell into a light sleep while the males celebrated.

Chapter Fourteen

ℬ

Every muscle in Marissa's body ached and throbbed as Kytar picked her up. A light touch in her mind lessened her soreness and as it decreased, she felt something else, something that wasn't hers. Her eyes widened as Kytar's satisfaction and pride and love came through clearly. Laughing, she nuzzled his throat, licking his salty warmth, feeling the strong beat of his pulse under her tongue. She felt his answering chuckle rumble through his chest.

* * * * *

"Our link has strengthened, just as the legends said it would."

"To the point that we can read each other's mind?" she questioned, even as she wanted to shout with joy. She felt their connection and knew herself cherished.

"You were warned about that. Many times, if I recall correctly," he said as he placed her on the bed.

She kept her arms wrapped around his neck and tilted her chin, inviting a kiss. *Now*, she thought. *Take me now. I can't wait any longer.*

He laughed and she heard his response in her head. *Amazing, isn't it? I'd heard stories, but I believed them exaggerated.*

She shuddered, in need, not fear. They'd gone far beyond fear. She couldn't deny her longing anymore. She needed him. She wanted him. She loved him. Reaching for his clothes, she helped him undress, desperate to feel his naked body next to hers.

153

He rubbed close while he stroked her with his hands, all over her body, lightly touching her. "You were magnificent. At times, I wondered if we'd survive. I'm very pleased with you."

Marissa expected to feel embarrassment, but realized she didn't. Instead, his words sent a thrill of accomplishment and pride singing through her body as she remembered the ritual. Thinking about it, she remembered her earlier question. "Why did it matter that you had never entered me?"

"The challenge ritual is a test, not of your responses, but of my strength. After collaring, the urge to consummate the binding is nearly irresistible. But you resisted and you were strong enough to challenge our binding. If I'd taken you before I met your challenge it would have proven that that I was not strong enough to hold you."

"So why was Talcor here during my training?"

"Talcor was my watcher," he murmured, kissing a line down her neck.

Knowing he was trying to distract her, she fought to focus. She'd hated having Talcor in the room, despite the fact he'd eventually helped her. She wanted to know why he'd been present during her training. "Watcher?" she asked.

Kytar pulled back until he could meet her eyes. "Training is dangerous. Talcor was there for two reasons. First, he was there to prevent me from breaching you prematurely. Had I done that, our link would have broken so violently that it could have meant death for one or both of us."

"And the second reason?"

Kytar made a move as if to get off the bed. Marissa placed her hand on his arm and felt his muscles tense as turmoil swirled within him.

"Kytar?"

His nostrils flared with his deep breath. "So I wouldn't hurt you beyond repair," he said, his voice husky. "Talcor was there to protect you from me."

Kytar's anguish caused tears to fill Marissa's eyes. His torment flooded her, but she didn't understand the reason for it. He'd calmed her enough times, could she now return the favor? She sent out her love and calming energies, trying to reach his mind.

A wry smile creased his face. "A Darinthian male cherishes his companion. There is an irresistible urge to protect her. It is unthinkable for a male to hurt his companion unless they've both agreed."

"But you told me I did agree when I challenged you."

"Yes. Your challenge gave me unlimited power over you and it short-circuited my natural inclination to protect you. It didn't remove it entirely, but it blunted it, making it possible for me to prepare you for the ritual. There were times when I was so angry with you..." he trailed off, staring into the distance before continuing. "I could have easily damaged you, seriously damaged you. Talcor was there to protect you."

"And you hate the fact another man had to protect me," said Marissa softly as she realized the source of Kytar's torment.

"You should never have to look to another man for protection."

Marissa hesitated, not sure how to help him. Then she remembered something he'd said early in their relationship. "You told me the collar is a symbol of protection, that if I wore a collar, I could call upon any man for help. How is that different than what Talcor did?"

"He had to protect you from me!"

"Only because I was foolish enough to challenge you," she retorted. "We both acted in ways we now regret. Let's forget the past," she said, reaching toward his lap. Rubbing his cock, feeling the steel beneath her hand, she coaxed it to its full height. "I need you."

Kytar chuckled, his tension changing from regret to need. He stroked Marissa's body, tingling warmth trailing his hand as he murmured, "The ritual was dangerous. I was terrified I'd lose you. Every man in the building expected you to lose control or me to lose control of you. You didn't, though. You accepted my touch. You were superb. I'm pleased that you were every bit as responsive as I hoped you'd be. You should be proud of yourself."

Marissa realized she was proud. Happy she'd pleased him, it had been a heady experience, almost as if she'd channeled the need of every man in the room. But she knew she hadn't done it alone. "And you should be proud of training me and proud of your strength." She grinned, knowing she didn't have to fight or pretend anymore and she'd never be alone again.

His lips grazed her forehead. "Your challenge failed, now you'll pay the penalty." He chuckled as he gathered her tight and kissed her, gently brushing his lips over hers. Slowly deepening the kiss, he worked his tongue between her lips, and into the hidden recesses of her mouth. Mimicking the act to come, his tongue went in and out, until she moaned. Holding her tight, controlling the kiss, he let her know that her pleasure was his to give or withhold.

He finally stopped torturing her mouth by moving his kiss across her chin, down her neck. Shivers of pleasure played along her spine. He continued with devoted attention across her breasts. Pausing a moment, he savored her nipples, licking each one before pulling and biting lightly.

Marissa shuddered as molten desire rushed to her belly and exploded outward. She moaned and tried to squirm, but his weight held her still.

Raising his head, he smiled down at her. "You understand now, don't you, little one?"

"Oh yes," she sighed, reaching for him but he stopped her with a quick motion.

Capturing her wrists in one hand, he raised them over her head and bound them.

"No," she moaned. "Let me touch you."

"Not yet." He smiled. Lowering himself, he spread her thighs. Holding her legs, he bent his head and parted her labia with a fingertip. Then he used both hands to open her wide.

She jumped when the tip of his tongue slowly and firmly licked her clitoris. Warmth curled outward. She clenched her thighs when he blew on her clit, but he held her exposed, open and helpless. Then a stroke moved in her head and she felt a lash across her buttocks. Lick, and then lash. Repeatedly, she bounced between physical pleasure and remembered pain. She moaned with the need generated by his cunning mixture of sensation until she could not tell one from the other.

He raised his head and held her eyes. Breezing through her mind were words. *I no longer need physically touch you.* His eyes glittered with satisfaction. Then it was as if his mouth touched her, laving her slit. All the while, his eyes held her and his mouth curved into a smile.

Fingers seemed to enter her cunt and spread her moisture. The movement merely increased her ache rather than soothing it. Lost in the sensations he effortlessly created in her mind, the throbbing need in her cunt held her captive.

"Please take me," she whispered, unable to speak louder through her need.

He laughed. "Not quite yet. Be still."

Marissa lost all sense of time. Sometimes he touched and sometimes he just used his mind. She couldn't tell which touch was physical and which was mental. Inside her head, they were the same. He pushed her further and proved she had no choice but to surrender her will to him.

"Please, please, please..." The words echoed in her head. She wasn't sure she spoke them or if he heard them. Either way, he ignored her pleading.

Fevered and writhing, she was lost in the wonder of her body until the tip of his cock paused at her entrance. Then she stilled, not daring to move, afraid he'd withdraw and leave her frustrated.

He framed her face with both his hands and forced her to meet his gaze. His eyes had turned a hard black. They held her for a long moment while he moved his hips forward.

The tip of his cock entered her dripping channel. She stopped breathing. He was so wide. The sheer size of his cock stretched her walls. Before she could panic, he smiled and started a relentless, agonizingly slow forward motion. He didn't stop again. He didn't hesitate or give her another chance to recover as he slowly, inexorably pushed forward, determinedly widening her narrow channel.

It seemed to take forever before he reached the end, but he kept moving forward. "It will stretch to take me all," she heard him murmur as she fought not to gasp that he was too big. He felt too good to stop, filling her with a pleasure she'd never dreamed possible. She gasped for air, trying to relax, trying to take all of him.

Split in two, her pussy burned as it adjusted to his girth. His presence in her mind helped her accept his size. He continued his pressure until she expanded to meet his full thickness and length.

She had fallen silent long before he finished seating himself fully within her body. Impaled on the length of his long member, his pelvis ground her hips into the bed. His pubic hair tickled her clitoris. She struggled to squirm, to move just a millimeter—she needed to move, but his full weight held her pinned.

Marissa surrendered to his domination and lay submissively under him, fully under his control. He rocked his pelvis a little, as if to make more room and her arousal rose to meet his movements. Thus, seated firmly, he grabbed her thighs and raised her legs over his shoulders, deepening his assault until he seemed to reach her throat. Then he stopped.

She clenched the cock buried deep inside. In response, he flexed his hips, nudging her cervix. When he pushed in even deeper, her arousal loosened her muscles just enough to give him another millimeter of depth.

"Tell me what you feel."

"You know what I feel," she said carelessly, bemused by sensation and not thinking.

He chuckled before touching a strand deep in her mind causing her nipples to remember the grip by the clamps. She gasped as the world blurred. She fought to reach the peak he held just out of reach.

"More," she groaned. "I need more, please..." she begged. He flexed his hips then stopped again.

"Stop teasing," she screamed.

He slowly withdrew until the tip of his cock just barely held her channel open, all the while keeping the circle of sensation going in her head. "Tell me what you need," he demanded.

"More, more, more," she heard herself mindlessly chant.

He laughed. "Not yet. We've waited too long for it to be over so soon."

She was wild, every muscle taut with need. She wanted him in every way he could take her. Still he wound the coil within her tighter and tighter.

He slammed back, using all his strength.

"Yesss," she hissed as he touched a core of need she'd never known existed. Kytar deepened his strokes. Her mind gave up its struggle for logic as he united them, mind and body, flooding her with his emotions.

She felt him teetering on the edge, barely holding on. Responding, she inundated him, demanding the satisfaction they both craved. His control broke under her onslaught of need. And they exploded into shards of light. Screaming with the agony and ecstasy of release as they finally consummated their binding.

* * * * *

Marissa awoke the next day sleepy-eyed and suffering from exhaustion, to find her father seated in a chair next to the bed.

As if he recognized her state, he smiled and kept his words soft. "I am proud of you. Your challenge ceremony will long be remembered."

Marissa waved a hand, barely hearing him as she wondered where Kytar had gone. She was still needy despite her recent satisfaction. But her father's next words startled her out of her passion-induced fog. "There's one more decision you have to make."

She groaned. "Enough," she said. "I'm tired of your rituals."

"Nonetheless, you will listen and answer," he replied.

She briefly closed her eyes and gritted her teeth. Where was Kytar? She should be able to feel him, shouldn't she? But it was as if he'd never been in her head. She didn't feel a trace of him. Opening her eyes, she nodded for her father to continue.

"You've earned the right to leave, if you choose to do so."

"What?" Her heart sank at his words. "What do you mean? My challenge failed, the link strengthened. I can't leave."

"Do you choose to leave?"

Marissa stared at him. Leave? Why would she leave? Her mind slipped to the pleasure of Kytar's body before she yanked her mind back to the present. Freedom, her father finally offered her freedom. She hesitated, but she couldn't say yes when she found herself reaching for Kytar, trying to sense his presence in the house. Nothing, she felt nothing. Where was he?

"What have you done with Kytar?"

"Kytar is not allowed to interfere with your choice," Davo said. "Do you choose to leave him?"

"Does he want me to leave?" Disappointment and emptiness caused her to blurt the question before she could stop herself.

Davo snorted, "Of course not. If he wanted you to leave he never would have bound you, trained you or faced the ritual with you, much less consummated your companionship."

Marissa couldn't prevent a sigh of relief.

"According to the rules of Darinth, you must answer me. Do you choose to leave?"

"But you told me the ritual bound us tighter. How can you offer to let me leave?"

"You are bound, but you were strong enough to challenge the link. You survived training and the ritual. That gives you the right to leave."

"You mean because I failed, I succeeded?" she asked slightly bewildered by this twist.

He nodded.

Marissa stared at her father. She wanted to scream in frustration. She'd thought she'd moved beyond the confusion of Darinthian rituals. His words made no sense but they must contain a hidden meaning. There was always a hidden meaning when the words got ritualistic. She tried to think it through. What was the catch?

"What happens if I leave?"

"Your bonds are dissolved."

"And that's it, nothing else?"

Her father's jaw tightened.

161

Then her heart stuttered. "Kytar — what happens to him?"

"I am not permitted to answer that question. Do you choose to leave?"

His ritualistic words sent a chill of fear rushing through her body and turmoil swirled in her brain. How many times had she cursed him and cursed Kytar? How many times had she begged for release? Now, freedom was hers. But release meant something bad for Kytar. She knew that, even if Davo wouldn't tell her what.

She closed her eyes, swamped by the memory of Kytar's lips and hands on her body, playing her like a fine instrument. Could she really walk away from the satisfaction he gave her, satisfaction far beyond anything she'd ever imagined possible? Even now, she longed to feel him. Where was he? Why wasn't he here to help her with this decision?

Then she realized she didn't need his help, not now. While she might not be enamored with the planet, she certainly didn't want to leave Kytar. He challenged her and satisfied her on so many levels. She simply couldn't bear the thought of leaving him.

Yes, his strength frightened her at times but it also lured and thrilled her, making her feel safe and protected. She belonged with him. Peace flooded her because this decision didn't have to be hard. For once, she'd take the easy route. Opening her eyes, she smiled and said, "I love Kytar. I will never leave him."

Her father sagged with relief. "The challenge is complete. Welcome to Darinth, daughter." Smiling, he held out an envelope. "Your mother left this letter for you," he said.

"What?" Marissa tried to form a coherent sentence. Drained from the past few weeks, the sudden call from the past shocked her. She hadn't expected any further communication from her mother. She looked at the small rectangular square of white. The last letter had changed her life. What would this one do? Her father left the room while she was still fixated on the paper he'd placed in her hand. Sighing, she broke the seal and read.

My darling,

I hope you don't hate me. If you are reading this letter, then you belong on Darinth. You've achieved a state that always frightened me. It frightened me so much that I ran from your father. I learned too late that I should have accepted his will and judgment. The binding frightened me and I gave in to fear. I am glad you are braver. Not a day has passed that I haven't regretted leaving your father. Not a day has passed that I haven't remembered him with longing. I was happy on Darinth. Perhaps by now you understand why. I hope you will forgive my earlier deception. I wanted you to have the opportunity to understand how freeing it is to be a companion, held safe by a strong man's arms. To know you are loved and protected frees you to love in return. I couldn't explain — you had to experience Darinth to understand. If I had told all at the beginning of your journey, would you have gone to Darinth? Enjoy your adventure.

All my love, always,

Mom

Tears streamed down Marissa's face. She remembered her mother's life and realized how much pain she must have hidden. Marissa's stepfather was a poor imitation of a Darinthian male. Her mother had suffered for turning her back on love.

Lost in her musings, Marissa hadn't seen Kytar enter the room. She felt him though as he gathered her into his arms. His mind played lightly over hers, easing her emotional pain. She sighed, content in his arms. She forgave her mother's deception.

She couldn't deny the deep satisfaction she felt with Kytar as he mentally reminded her of the power of their link.

* * * * *

The next day, Marissa's hands shook as she tried to brush her hair. This was silly, she told herself. She shouldn't be more frightened of meeting her family than she had been by the challenge ritual. But her stomach clenched into a tight knot that refused to relax.

Kytar came up behind her and took the brush from her hand. Soothing her turmoil, he said, "They are just as excited to meet you as you are to meet them. They are family and family is sacred on Darinth. Otherwise, the council wouldn't have agreed that you meet them before we go into isolation and consolidate our bonds. You needn't stress over this encounter."

She sighed with relief as he stroked her thoughts, soothing the rough edges, replacing her anxiety with excitement. She leaned back against his broad chest as his arms came around her and he kissed her hair.

"We have to leave if we're to be on time."

Feeling more secure, she nodded. "Let's go."

Kytar held her close as he led her to her father's house. They walked through the door into a crowd of a hundred people. Her eyes widened, these were all relatives? Before she had a chance to panic, Davo spotted her and came over.

Grabbing her hand, he said, "Come, it is long past time for you to meet your relatives." And he led her into the welcoming crowd.

Also by Cyna Kade

ଔ

eBooks:

Linking Shelley

Mastering Marissa

Power and Pain 1: Releasing Kate

Power and Pain 2: Outside Sanctuary

Power and Pain 3: Inside Sanctuary

Stripped by Love

Tessa's Ambassador

About the Author

ଛଏ

Cyna Kade started reading science fiction and fantasy when she was ten. By age fifteen, she added romance to her reading list. Erotica followed much later. Cyna believes the best books mix genres and she's followed that belief in her life. She's lived in north, east, south and west. She's been married and liberated and deeply loves her children. She's worked as an x-ray tech, a computer programmer, a systems analyst, a university instructor and earned a multidisciplinary Ph.D. Hobbies are equally varied, including stained glass and tai chi.

ଛଏ

The author welcomes comments from readers. You can find her website and email address on her author bio page at www.ellorascave.com.

Tell Us What You Think

We appreciate hearing reader opinions about our books. You can email us at Comments@EllorasCave.com.

Why an electronic book?

We live in the Information Age—an exciting time in the history of human civilization, in which technology rules supreme and continues to progress in leaps and bounds every minute of every day. For a multitude of reasons, more and more avid literary fans are opting to purchase e-books instead of paper books. The question from those not yet initiated into the world of electronic reading is simply: *Why?*

1. *Price.* An electronic title at Ellora's Cave Publishing runs anywhere from 40% to 75% less than the cover price of the exact same title in paperback format. Why? Basic mathematics and cost. It is less expensive to publish an e-book (no paper and printing, no warehousing and shipping) than it is to publish a paperback, so the savings are passed along to the consumer.

2. *Space.* Running out of room in your house for your books? That is one worry you will never have with electronic books. For a low one-time cost, you can purchase a handheld device specifically designed for e-reading. Many e-readers have large, convenient screens for viewing. Better yet, hundreds of titles can be stored within your new library—on a single microchip. There are a variety of e-readers from different manufacturers. You can also read e-books on your PC or laptop computer. (Please note that Ellora's Cave does not endorse any specific brands.

You can check our website at www.ellorascave.com for information we make available to new consumers.)

3. *Mobility.* Because your new e-library consists of only a microchip within a small, easily transportable e-reader, your entire cache of books can be taken with you wherever you go.

4. *Personal Viewing Preferences.* Are the words you are currently reading too small? Too large? Too... ANNOYING? Paperback books cannot be modified according to personal preferences, but e-books can.

5. *Instant Gratification.* Is it the middle of the night and all the bookstores near you are closed? Are you tired of waiting days, sometimes weeks, for bookstores to ship the novels you bought? Ellora's Cave Publishing sells instantaneous downloads twenty-four hours a day, seven days a week, every day of the year. Our webstore is never closed. Our e-book delivery system is 100% automated, meaning your order is filled as soon as you pay for it.

Those are a few of the top reasons why electronic books are replacing paperbacks for many avid readers.

As always, Ellora's Cave welcomes your questions and comments. We invite you to email us at Comments@ellorascave.com or write to us directly at Ellora's Cave Publishing Inc., 1056 Home Avenue, Akron, OH 44310-3502.

ELLORA'S CAVE
Romanticon

Annual convention
for women who
refuse to behave

Lightning Source UK Ltd.
Milton Keynes UK
UKOW051728190911

178922UK00001B/119/P